CALVIN

THE BROTHERS OF HASTINGS RANCH SERIES
BOOK TWO

By Katharine E. Hamilton

ISBN-13: 978-0-578-71087-7

Calvin

www.katharinehamilton.com

Cover Design by Kerry Prater.

To Everett and West.
My little cowboys.

Acknowledgments

Thanks to my cover designer, Kerry Prater, for helping me search for the perfect picture of Calvin. We actually designed a completely different cover for Calvin and scratched it based on my husband's feedback. In the end, I feel we truly captured Calvin, and this cover turned out awesome.

Thank you to my editor, Lauren Hanson. She is always on board when I email her a final draft and say, "Hey, can you do this in 3 days?" Ha! I hope to not make a habit of it. Thank you, Lauren!

My husband, Brad. It's fun tossing ideas off of you. I also love watching you work. There's nothing more attractive than a man who knows what he's doing and loves doing it. (Siiiiigh)

Dr. Jan Pol, veterinarian, for giving me the information I needed for technical jargon in regards to Alice's line of work.

To my son, Everett, for his patience, not only with me bringing a new baby brother home in the midst of writing this book, but for also his loving nature towards Momma working more to wrap up this book in the midst of bringing home Baby West. You're a champ, E.

H

Chapter One

"*I don't see why* we need such a fancy filing system," Alice Wilkenson complained as she handed another patient file to her best friend, Julia. Julia had moved from Santa Fe a little over three weeks prior and had already begun her organizing and revamping of the veterinary clinic Alice and her dad had run together for years. Not that she didn't appreciate her friend's efforts. Of course, she did. She just didn't like learning something new. That took time. Time Alice didn't have.

"A spreadsheet corresponding with the filing shelves in the back is not fancy. It's smart." Julia motioned to the filing cabinet. "Besides, I will be the one mostly filing things away, this is just so you know what's going on and where things are. This filing cabinet cannot hold thirty years' worth of files." Julia flipped open a chart. "This pet, if it were still alive, would be twenty-seven years old. I don't think I've ever met a twenty-seven-year-old Labrador. Have you?" Julia tossed the file to a stack on the side. "It can be filed in the back."

"I see your point," Alice grumbled. "Just keep it simple, please. I don't have the brain capacity to take on yet another thing right now."

"That is why *I'm* doing it, and why *I'm* here. To help." Julia smiled encouragingly. "Any news from Philip?"

Alice shook her head. She hadn't expected any news from the Hastings brother. She'd just posted the flyer seeking another veterinarian two days ago, though Julia thought Alice had taken care of it weeks prior. She left that part out as she shrugged. "We'll see if anyone bites."

"Well, I told Graham to mention it at his conference this weekend."

"I'll cross my fingers."

"He said he would," Julia defended.

"If Graham speaks to anyone at conferences, I would be shocked."

"He's leading a seminar," Julia proudly stated. "So obviously people value what my man has to say."

"Oh, I bet that's a real exciting session." Alice smirked but then tapped her knuckles on the counter. "I'm just giving you a hard time. I know Graham is well-respected. All the brothers are. I just like to hear you defend him." She winked. "So, you almost at a stopping point? I'm ready to head out."

"Sure. Let me just *file this away*." Julia tucked the stack of files into a box next to her feet and carried it towards the back of the clinic. Alice followed, watching as her friend slid the labeled box onto the shelf with corresponding label. Julia was definitely better at organizing than she was. Alice had absolutely no desire to do what her friend was doing. She did value it, though, because just in the few short weeks Julia had been at the clinic, everything ran more smoothly. Since Alice was the only vet at the moment, Julia restructured her day for pet appointments at the clinic in the morning and house call appointments in the afternoon, unless an emergency popped up. She also noticed an ad in the Sheffield paper that boasted not only the flyer for their need of another vet, but also a vet technician. Julia must have added that. Smart move. Alice would almost settle for anyone with the proper training at this point, just to get some help.

Julia reappeared, pumped some hand sanitizer on her hands, and then grabbed her purse. "Ready."

"Did you make dinner plans with Graham already?"

"No. I actually haven't talked to him since this morning. I think he and Calvin were to be on equipment most of the day."

"Ah... so he's going to be a real peach this evening." Alice rolled her eyes. "Maybe we can just do our own thing then. Leave him a plate in the oven. Because both Cal and Graham don't know when to call it quits when they're on equipment. They'll push until the last ray of sun disappears and then some."

"You're probably right. He mentioned something about a fence line, and he didn't sound too excited about it. We could eat at Ruby's."

"Sloppy's?" Alice tilted her head as she considered it. "I could go for a good chicken fried steak."

"Then it's settled. And would it be so hard to call her Ruby instead of Sloppy?" Julia asked.

"Old habits are hard to break."

"Still, she's our friend." Julia slid into the passenger side of Alice's truck, the door creaking as she closed it.

Alice, like a blaze of fury, backed out of the parking lot and began speeding her way towards

Parks. The usual drive only took half the time with her behind the wheel. She wasn't much for driving slowly, or the speed limit for that matter, if she could set her own pace, that's how she liked it. And thankfully, growing up and working in the area of her childhood, local law enforcement didn't seem to pay her any mind. Though she would be pulled over by a new recruit on occasion, but Judge Iverson pardoned her each and every time. Thank God for Annie and Henry being his next-door neighbors and Alice benefiting from that relationship.

Julia's phone rang and she flashed a pleased smile before answering and a deep voice muttered on the other end. Alice immediately knew it was Graham.

"I was hoping to hear from you," Julia beamed. "Long day?"

Alice focused on the turn ahead into Sloppy's parking lot and pulled up front. They were a bit early for the supper rush, but she didn't care. She was thirsty and felt like she could eat her weight in chicken fried steak. Part of that was due to the lunch hour she neglected. Julia had taken it upon herself to pack their lunches each morning, but no matter how hard Alice tried, she just couldn't muster up excitement for an egg salad sandwich earlier in the day. So she chugged another coke and went about her day. Now, sitting and waiting for Julia to finish her conversation in the car, all she could think about were creamy mashed potatoes smothered in white gravy and an ice-cold sweet tea. Her mouth watered as she offered a wave towards Roughneck Randy sitting by the entrance.

"Yes, we're eating at Ruby's. I guess I will see you later tonight then. Call me if you change your mind." She hung up. "Graham said not to worry about food for them. He was just going to grab a sandwich or something."

"Works for me." Alice hopped out of her car quicker than a prairie dog and scurried towards the door. She patted Randy on the shoulder as she passed. Sloppy, or Ruby, as was her real name, stood behind the bar and smiled.

"Ladies night, hm?"

"Something like that." Alice pointed to a table. "We're starving."

"Be right over." Ruby waved at Julia as she grabbed a couple of menus and brought them to the table. "You two are hardly without a Hastings these days. Are the boys in the doghouse?"

Julia shook her head. "No, just busy. I'm starting to understand the long days of ranch life."

"She's depressed because she didn't receive flirty texts from Graham all day."

Ruby chuckled. "Does Graham even send flirty texts? That's hard to imagine."

Julia flushed. "Well, not flirty. More like sweet. He sends a lot of 'I'm thinking of you' messages."

"Now that is sweet and hard to envision." Ruby grinned. "What can I get you ladies?"
Alice placed her order and then rolled her eyes as Julia ordered a salad.

"I'll bring you guys an appetizer to get you started."

"You're a lifesaver." Alice sighed as Ruby hustled away and rushed back with two glasses of sweet tea before wandering back into the kitchen. Though she had a cook, Sal, Ruby liked to be hands-on when she had the time. And since Alice and Julia were the only two people in the place, Alice knew Ruby was back there, hand-battering her steak on her own. "So, for the weekend I was thinking we could—" Her words trailed off as she glanced out the window. "Are you kidding me?" She stood to her feet and darted out the door before Julia could respond.

"What's with her?" Ruby placed a tray of chips and salsa in front of Julia.

"I have no idea." The two women peered out the window and when Alice stepped back from her truck, they saw the problem. Her front left tire was flat.

Alice stormed back inside and pulled out her cell phone. "Hey, it's me. You wouldn't be in town, would you? I have a flat over at Slop's." She groaned. "Right, okay. Thanks." She hung up. "Philip is out at the ranch helping the guys draft fence plans, so he can't change my tire." She scrolled through her phone.

"I'm sure we could change it," Julia replied encouragly, and Ruby nodded in agreement.

Skeptical, Alice looked at the two women. "Have you ever changed a tire?"

"Once." Julia took a sip of her tea. "When I was sixteen. My dad taught me. I'm sure it's not difficult."

"Besides," Ruby grinned. "we're tough women. We don't need a Hastings brother to bail us out."

"I suppose you're right." Alice frowned at her phone. "You know what, you *are* right. I have gotten so dependent on them it's almost sickening. After we eat, we'll give it a go."

"Right on." Ruby pumped a fist in the air. "I'll go check your order." She hopped away, her bright purple sneakers squeaking across the floor.

"I think she's excited to get some fresh air." Julia grinned. "We'll show those Hastings men we are more than capable of changing a tire."

"I hope you're right," Alice sighed as she dipped a chip in salsa. "The last thing I need is Calvin Hastings on my case about my truck again."

"He nags because he cares," Julia pointed out.

"That he does," Alice laughed. "Sometimes a little too much. And it is not out of care for me, but for the vehicle."

"I think that's only partially true," Julia added. "All those Hastings boys love their Alice."

Alice fluffed her hair. "You bet they do. I'm the only woman that could tolerate them before you came along. They owe me."

Laughing, Julia shook her head and accepted her plate of salad from Ruby while Alice leaned forward and inhaled a deep whiff of her meal before eagerly diving into her dish.

"Tomorrow we'll start pulling wire off." Graham tossed his empty thermos into the bed of his truck as he spoke to his younger brothers, all corralled around the back end of the vehicle to plan for the next day's events.

"I don't get why we can't just bulldoze it all?" Seth, the youngest Hastings brother, pulled his cowboy hat from his head to wipe away the sweat on his brow. "I mean, Gramps is the one who built this thing when he was our age. It's old. Too many patch jobs to even consider repairing it."

"The posts are still good," Calvin explained.

"And the hard part is over," Graham continued.

"So you say," Clint, one of the other brothers sighed. "You're not the one that has to pull up posts."

"Hey, Graham and I were on equipment all day making a path for you. Not even a thank you?" Calvin looked to Graham with mock bewilderment. "Ungrateful pinhead."

"Just saying, I think we are wasting time on this project," Clint continued.

"You won't think that when we are able to expand our grazing grounds." Lawrence nodded his dimpled chin towards his older brothers to continue. Never one to shy away from hard work, Calvin appreciated Lawrence's support.

"Hayes?" Graham asked. "Everyone else seems to have an opinion. What about you?"

Hayes pointed to Philip. "He hadn't said anything either."

"Well, Philip is making money off of this project, so I know he's not going to complain," Graham pointed out and his brother nodded with a smirk.

Hayes shrugged his shoulders. "It needs to be done. I say we do it. We've laid the groundwork already, or Calvin has anyway, by clearing the fence line. Though I hate summer projects, we can't leave this fence like it is if we plan to use this pasture."

"Agreed." Graham nodded his dismissal of everyone and watched as his brothers tiredly dragged their feet towards their trucks or horses.

"They're going to complain the entire time," Calvin chuckled. "Allllllll summer long. You ready for that?"

"We can take 'em."

Calvin laughed. "True. Clint and Seth are going to lag, mostly on purpose."

"That's why I think they'd be great working with Lawrence. He won't let them."

"Possibly." Calvin scratched his stubbled chin. He started the day off with his natural sandy blonde hair and by the end of the day, due to all the dirt, sweat, and grime, his whiskers always seemed to turn a darker shade of brown.

Philip walked up carrying a clipboard.

"Once we pull the posts tomorrow, I'll be able to give you better numbers." Graham pulled his gloves from his back pocket and stuffed them into his tool chest.

Philip, tapping his pen on the clipboard, nodded. "This gives me at least an idea. I'll look tomorrow at costs and let you know. Same with wire."

"Yeah, definitely going to need all new wire," Calvin added. "I'm surprised this old fence held up as long as it has."

"Credit to the builders," Graham stated, acknowledging their grandfather's hard work. "I'll give you the numbers tomorrow," Graham repeated. "Right now, I'm dead on my feet."

"Likewise." Calvin pointed towards his truck. "I want to go home and have a hot shower and a cold meal."

"Speaking of meals," Philip slipped his pen behind his ear. "Alice called me from Sloppy's. Said she had a flat tire."

Calvin rolled his eyes heavenward. "Probably drove it down to the rim too."

"Don't know. Just thought I'd let you guys know. She and Julia were going to eat supper there and then head back. If all else fails, Randy could change it for them."

"Roughneck Randy?" Calvin shook his head. "No way. Look, I love Randy, but he doesn't know up from down most days." He looked to Graham. "You talked to Julia?"

"Earlier. They were about to pull into Slop's. Guess she didn't know about the tire yet."

"Looks like I'm headed into town here in a bit." Calvin wiped a palm over his tired face.

"Just let them sort it out," Philip said. "They're grown women, and there are plenty of people in town who can help them out. Besides, they may already be on their way home by the time you even reach the house."

Knowing he was over an hour away from his hot shower and cold supper, Calvin saw the logic of Philip's response. However, he also knew Alice. And if Randy offered, she'd take the first and easiest option to fix the tire, even if it was the worst decision. "I'll call her and see."

Graham nodded as he loaded up into his truck, completely unphased by the dilemma. Calvin thought his brother would be speeding towards town for Julia, considering the woman had completely altered his brother's brain chemistry over the last few months, but surprisingly, Graham headed towards his house.

Calvin reached for his cell phone and dialed Alice. She answered in a huff of exertion.

"To what do I owe the pleasure, Cal?" Alice grunted as Julia's voice could be heard in the background issuing directions.

"Lefty loosey, Alice." Julia, sounding frustrated, was echoed by the sound of the lug wrench hitting the ground.

"Then you have at it," Alice huffed, as the phone shifted and she turned her attention back to Cal.

"Philip said you girls have a flat."

"We do, but nothing we can't handle."

"Sounds like it."

"Did you call to tease us or were you planning a daring rescue? Either way, not needed."

"You sure?" He softened his tone. Alice sounded at her wits' end and the last thing he wanted was to add to the stress of her situation.

"I'm sure. We've got this."

"Alright. Well, call if you need me to dart up."

"Doubtful, but thanks."

He pulled the phone away from his ear and stuffed it into his shirt pocket. He debated whether he should head up to Sloppy's anyway or let Alice and Julia figure out the tire on their own. He didn't like it, but he decided to give them a little leeway. He'd let them try to change the tire. If they needed help, he or Graham would get a phone call, he was sure of it. So he'd stick with his plan to head home and shower. Something in his gut told him not to get too comfortable at home, though he hoped he was wrong.

ℋ

Chapter Two

"Was that Calvin?" Julia looked up from her squatting position beside the tire.

"Yep. Offering to save us." Alice rolled her eyes. "How's it coming down there?"

"Taking it off now." Julia hefted the tire and lifted it off the frame and hoisted it aside. "Your turn."

"What am I supposed to do?" Alice asked. "Looks to me like you've got the hang of this."

"You can put the new tire on." Julia motioned to the spare resting against the back tire as she wiped a dirty hand across her forehead.

"But you're doing such a great job." Alice groaned

and rolled her eyes as Julia crossed her arms in annoyance. "Fine. I'll do it."

"Thank you, Julia, for helping me," Julia quipped. "You're such a great friend. I'm so glad you know how to change a tire. Sure is helpful."

"Yeah, yeah, yeah." Alice grinned as she rolled the spare into position and hefted it onto the rim.

Ruby walked out with two to-go cups, handing one to Julia and resting the other on the hood of the truck for Alice. "You girls are rockin' it. Thought you might need some refreshment. Well, you and Roughneck Randy." She nodded towards the old man sitting by the entrance of her restaurant and he waved with a cheerful smile. "He said you girls should start your own mechanic shop."

"He could get up off his rear end and help," Alice grumbled.

"You know he can't, with his bad back and all," Ruby defended.

"So he says," Alice continued.

Julia waved away her comment as she took a sip of her drink. "Thanks, Ruby."

"Don't mention it. You girls text me when you

make it back to the ranch safely."

"Will do." Julia smiled as their spunky friend darted back inside with a quick and friendly tap to Randy's shoulder on her way.
"I got it." Alice stood and tossed the lug wrench into the bed of her truck. "And just like that we are back on the road."

"Good. I'm beat." Julia walked to the passenger side and slid into the truck as Alice tossed one last wave towards Randy before hopping behind the wheel and cranking the engine.

"So, tomorrow I'll be out of the office most of the day. I set the phone line to divert to your cell if you don't feel like driving to Sheffield."

"Sounds good to me. It will be nice to have a day at the house and continue to settle in. I still have a few boxes I haven't unpacked yet." Julia glanced at her watch. "And I doubt I will do any of it this evening. I'm ready to see Graham and visit with him."

Alice smirked. "Oh, Graham... the romantic."

"Don't poke fun." Julia grinned. "He actually is sometimes, you know."

"Oh, I know. Now. He softens up when he sets eyes on you."

"As it should be," Julia stated proudly.

"True. If any of the brothers are needing a task tomorrow, have them check the leak in the refrigerator. I told Graham about it, but if it's not ranch-related he tends to forget about it."

"When did the fridge start leaking?" Julia asked.

"Noticed it this morning."

"You could have told me," Julia chuckled. "I could have followed up with him throughout the day until one of the brothers took a look at it."

Alice waved away her concern. "They'll get to it."

"This is how your other house fell into disrepair," Julia sighed. "You're too lackadaisical about things. Soon it will be weeks before it's checked."

"Not with you around. I told you now, so I know you will see that it gets taken care of as well. See? I'm not completely apathetic."

Alice navigated around a carcass in the middle of the road and hit a small pothole for her trouble, but continued on her way towards the 7H Ranch. Twenty miles outside of Parks, Texas, the ranch had been in the Hastings family for generations. She felt her truck shift towards the left and corrected her course. Glancing out her window towards the troublesome tire, her eyes widened. She flicked her turn signal on and pulled over to the side of the road.

"What's going on?" Julia asked.

"The tire."

"What's wrong with it?"

"It's loose or something."

"Did you tighten the lug nuts all the way?"

"I thought I did. I just want to check it." Alice slipped out and peered down at the problem. Sighing, she pulled her phone from her pocket.

"You back?" Cal's voice rang through the line.

"Not quite. Almost." She ran a hand through her hair, disappointed in herself that she had to ask him for help. "I have a question for you."

"Shoot," he said, and she could hear him step out onto his front porch, the familiar slapping sound of his screen door closing behind him.

"If a tire loses a few lug nuts, is it still okay to drive on it?"

"How many we talking about?"

"Umm..."

"Alice," His tone grew frustrated. "where you at?"

"Just around the big bend in the road."

"I'll be there in a few minutes."

She hung up and hopped back into the air-conditioned interior.

"I take it we need a rescue?" Julia asked.

"Unfortunately."

"We aren't that far," Julia encouraged. "So maybe it won't take him too long."

"It's Cal. He drives like a grandma."

"Then why didn't you call one of the other guys?" Julia asked.

Alice shrugged and missed the sly smile Julia cast her way. Though Calvin was known for his slow driving, it wasn't but ten minutes later that he was pulling up to help them. He'd showered, she noticed, and he wore his "at home" clothes instead of his usual work jeans and button up. Instead, his shirt was a simple cotton t-shirt, that showcased his physique in ways she'd never acknowledged before. She hadn't ever seen him dressed outside of church and work clothes. Well, except when they were kids. Comfortable Cal was quite appealing. She shook away the thought as he neared the window. She rolled it down. "Thanks for coming."

"Glad you girls made it this far. You're missing some lug nuts. Good thing you noticed. If you hadn't pulled over and lost the rest the tire would have left the rim. Could have been a bad accident. Julia." He tilted his head in greeting towards the other side of the vehicle."

"Hey, Cal. Thanks for coming to help."

"No problem. I'm going to rearrange some of your lug nuts from the other tires to share with this one to get you ladies home. But tomorrow you'll need to pick some up at the auto parts store, or I can. Either way, you don't need to be driving this truck without them."

"I have house calls to make all day tomorrow." Alice shook her head. "I have to have my truck."

"You can take Shirley."

"I'm not taking your old, beat up pickup."

"She runs ten times better than this one." Cal

patted the windowsill. "And she has all her lug nuts."

"And she also moves like a snail."

"Only because I drive the speed limit. Look, let's just get you ladies home and we can argue about it there. I'll follow behind." His boots crunched along the gravel back towards his truck and Alice scoffed before shaking her head in annoyance.

"Why does everything have to be an argument with him?" she vented. "He's always nitpicking my truck, my house, my work. I'm getting 'bout tired of it."

"I think it's just his way of seeing about you," Julia explained. "He wants to help you, but you're too stubborn to accept help. So if he acts like it annoys him to help you, then maybe you'd be more open to it."

"I accept help," Alice defended. "I just don't like to be scolded every other breath."

Julia bit back a grin as she glanced into the sideview mirror of the passenger side and saw Cal talking on his cell phone, no doubt already calling the auto parts store on her friend's behalf.

∞

True to his word, the next morning Cal

parked Shirley in front of the guest house for Alice to use. He even transferred all of her vet equipment and bags so that when she woke up, she was ready to hit the road. Julia stepped out onto the porch and waved, her coffee cup in her hand, as she started her walk towards Graham's house. They'd share in their morning cup of coffee on the porch of the main house, and then his older brother would set out for work. It was a nice, new routine for Graham, and Calvin appreciated Julia more and more each day as Graham's once stern approach to life slowly softened bit by bit.

"Morning, Cal," she greeted. "Need some coffee?"

"Mornin'." He tipped his hat. "I'm good. Got a thermos full waiting for me at the house."

"And how are you getting back to your house?" Julia asked, pointing at Shirley.

"Just going to take a nice walk this morning."

Julia's brows rose, knowing it was just over a mile back to his place, she opened her mouth to comment, but stopped. Instead, she smiled. "You spoil her, you know."

He rubbed the back of his neck and flushed. It wasn't that he meant to spoil Alice, or that he even tried to, it was just... Alice. She'd always been there for them. Always. When their parents passed away, she was the only friend who didn't tip-toe around them. She was there. Sturdy. Solid. And Alice never let up, still teased them relentlessly. A friend. And he felt inclined to make sure he was always there for her in return. Perhaps he did tend to her more than his other brothers. But in his defense, most of her issues involved machines, and he was the machine guy. He liked working with his hands on equipment of all shapes, sizes, and functions.

"I didn't mean to embarrass you," Julia continued. "Just think it is sweet that you look out for her. She needs it sometimes, even if she won't admit it."

"She'll be mad as a hornet when she sees I've touched her stuff."

Julia chuckled as she nodded. "Yes. Yes, she will. But she will also quickly get over it. That's her way." She toasted her mug towards him as she hurried towards Graham's. Just then, the screen door of the guesthouse opened and a disheveled Alice glowered at him.

"I told you I'm not driving that." Alice, barefoot, hands on hips, and fluffy, night hair, stormed down into the yard towards him.

"You are." Cal kept his voice calm. "I even transferred everything over so you can be on your way when… well, when you clean up."

"What's wrong with the way I look?" Alice, offended, crossed her arms over her chest.

Cal bit back a laugh. "Well, you're in your pajamas, Al. I doubt you plan on makin' house calls like that." He watched as some of the heat faded from her blue eyes.

"Fine." She huffed her bangs out of her eyes and then used one hand to tuck them behind her ears. "I'll take Shirley. I'll get more lug nuts while I'm in town."

"Already called and they'll have them ready for you."
She tilted her head at him and squinted her eyes to study him. "That was generous."

"I figured it would be helpful in the midst of your busy day."

"I guess it is." She sighed and dropped her arms. "Fine. Thank you."

He smirked. "See, that wasn't so hard, was it?" He tugged on the edge of her hair. "Let me know when you bring her home." He patted Shirley's hood as he started walking towards his own house.

"You are seriously walking home?"

"Gotta get my work truck," he called over his shoulder.

"Well, give me a sec and I'll give you a ride."

"That hair is going to take more than a sec." He grinned as he walked backwards just to see her annoyed expression and the flustered movement of her trying to tame it beneath her fingers.

"Jerk!" she called.

"You ol' bitty!" he fired back, and he saw the smile she flashed before scurrying back into the guesthouse to ready herself for the day.

He was saved about a half mile from his house when Graham rolled by him, rolling down his window. "Get in. I'll give you a lift the rest of the way."

"Thanks." Calvin hopped inside the truck.

"Al make a fuss about Shirley?"

"No more than she normally would."

"Good deal."

"So we ready to pull wire?" Calvin asked.

"I hope so. Lawrence headed out early this

morning with Seth hoping to pull as much as they could before the heat sets in later."

"Bet Seth loved the wake-up call." Calvin grinned.

"Well, until he gets his house built, he's at Lawrence's beck and call." Graham shrugged his shoulders. "I'll just be impressed if Clint shows up early."

"Yeah. What are we going to do with him? He's been quite... well, unreliable."

"I've been thinking on that. Talked with Philip. He could use some help at the store. Thought about making him drive into to town and help there for a week or so, see how he does. If he likes it, Philip said he's got space for him. If he hates it, then maybe he'll appreciate working closer to home here."

"You'd honestly let him leave the ranch for work?"

"I have no control over any of you," Graham stated. "Y'all are free to leave whenever you want."

"I didn't mean that you kept us here. I just meant can we afford to lose him?"

"What worth is he to us if he doesn't show up for work or does a halfhearted job on everything he does?"

"True," Calvin agreed.

"Truth is, I'm tired of fightin' him. If he wants to try something else, so be it. But I'm tired of having to babysit."

"Guess we'll see how he does today." Calvin hopped out of Graham's truck and into his own as soon as Graham pulled to a stop.

"Coffee," Graham reminded him.

Calvin snapped his fingers and quickly darted into his house to grab his thermos. He definitely wouldn't make it far in the morning without a strong brew churning through his system. And as he saw Clint's truck slowly making its way towards the pasture they aimed to work in for the day, he knew he'd need the entire thermos just to make it through the first hour of arguments between Clint and Graham

H

Chapter Three

It was the second call of the day and Alice found herself winding her way through Sheffield towards Rankin. The Mayfield Farm had been one of her father's clients for over twenty-five years. The dairy farm boasted 2800 cows and nearly 20 employees and it operated around the clock. She was no stranger to dairies. Though she tended more to cattle ranches or horses when it came to large animals, every now and then a call would come in from Mayfield and off she'd go. They had options when it came to vets, but their loyalty to her father tended to win out most days, and so she didn't mind traveling a bit further north to see to their herd.

Today, she braced herself for what Jake, the foreman, believed were two left-displaced abomasum cases, a serious and potentially deadly scenario for a cow. Dairy cows were too precious a commodity for the farmer not to call a vet to come check it out. She pulled up in record time, Shirley moving faster than Alice thought her capable. As she shut her door, Jake sauntered up, hat in hand.

"Ms. Alice, thanks for comin' so quickly."

"No problem. How are they doing?"

"Not too good. We've got them separated out over here." He led the way to a small hay barn away from the main milking barn and operation headquarters. "I'm hoping it's just LDA," he continued. "but we've never had two at a time like this."

"We'll see what we've got," Alice encouraged. "No sense panicking before we know for sure."

He nodded in agreement as she walked into the barn. Jake had already lined up five of his strongest men to help her if she needed to treat for LDA, *that* she appreciated.

Alice stepped into the pen and gently ran her hand over the first downed cow's hide in a soothing gesture. She thumped her fingers over the cow's belly until a solid thunk sounded. "Yep. Hear that?" She thumped it several times. "Definitely a displaced abomasum. Let's get her flipped over." She took a step back so the men could ease the cow over onto her back, the process taking a good ten minutes even with the strength from the men involved. Cows did not and were not meant to lie on their backs and it was always a struggle to get them to do so.

Alice, not big on unnecessary surgeries in LDA circumstances, readied a toggle. She waited for the stomach to float back into the correct position and then stitched the toggle in the stomach to the lining of the abdomen to hold it in place. "Got it." She backed up and watched as the men eased the cow back to her stomach and helped her rise to her feet. "Give her a few days," Alice told Jake. "Make sure it doesn't relapse, but she looks good." Alice patted the cow's side. Swiping an arm over her forehead, she looked to Jake. "Where's the next one?"

It was close to lunchtime when she'd finished up at Mayfield's. After the two LDA procedures, she'd made the rounds to check on new calves and other concerns before heading out. She glanced at her clock on the dashboard of Shirley. Reaching for her phone, she dialed Julia to let her know she'd wrapped up at Mayfield's.

"I'm surprised to be hearing from you so soon," Julia's voice flooded over the line.

"Just a couple of LDAs and then some standard checkups."

"What's an LDA?"

"Are you about to eat lunch?"

"I am." Julia's voice pitched up in excitement. "Graham is pulling up the drive as we speak."

"Then I'll save you the details of an LDA for later," Alice chuckled, knowing Julia's weak stomach would appreciate the delay.

"Got it. Where are you headed next? You've got the call out at the Weatherfords' at two. Don't forget."

"Yeah, it'll take me the next couple of hours to get over there, so I'm going to grab some fast food and just head that way. Any more calls come in?"

"Not for on call. Most are just scheduling for tomorrow or later this week at the clinic. By the way, do you treat rats?"

Alice grinned. "Yes, unfortunately."

"Gross," Julia gagged. "I'll call her back then. A lady was wanting you to see her pet rat, but I wasn't sure if you did. I'll schedule her down for some time tomorrow."

"Most rats involve tumors. I'm sure that's what it is."

"Gross." Julia repeated. "I'm about to eat Alice. I don't want to talk about rat tumors."

"Rat tumors?" Graham's voice echoed in the background and Alice could just envision Julia waving him off as she continued her conversation.

"Let me know when you're done at Weatherford's. Unless an emergency comes in, that should be your last call of the day. I wasn't sure how long it would take you, so I didn't schedule anything else."

"You're a good woman, Julia McComas."

"I like to think so," Julia laughed. "Be careful. Drive safely. Don't want to crash Shirley in a rush."

"I'd never hear the end of it," Alice agreed. "I'll call you later. Tell Graham he's a butthead."

"What? Why?"

"Just because." Alice shrugged her shoulders as if she needed a reason and then smiled as Julia reported her message.

"He said it takes one to know one," Julia replied with a long-suffering sigh. "Honestly, you're like children."

Laughing, Alice hung up, grateful her friend seemed to embrace the odd and quirky relationship she had with the Hastings brothers. She loved them like family. And like family, she loved to nag and pick on them. And vice versa. Stomach grumbling, she spotted a burger joint off the highway and immediately directed her way there.

∞

"I still don't see why we can't just doze it all. This has taken forever." Seth swiped a hand through sweaty hair before settling his hat back in place. His face, streaked with dirt and sweat, mirrored the other brothers' as they all walked towards their vehicles to call it a day. A long day. A hard day.

"We want the posts," Calvin reminded him. "And the brush is a hindrance. Navigating a dozer around the posts and brush doesn't make sense."

"My hands were crampin' up there towards the end." Lawrence held his gloved hands in front of him and flexed his fingers. "I hate pulling staples."

"Julia's at the house." Graham's hard tone cut through their complaining. "If you need a tenderhearted woman to whine to, I'm sure she'll listen."

"Not whining," Lawrence pointed out. "Just stating a fact."

"That you're gettin' old," Calvin teased.

"Right. You're older than I am, bro."

"Ah, but my hands aren't cramping up on me."

"I think I didn't drink enough water or somethin'."

"Well, I'm whinin'," Seth admitted. "And not ashamed about it."

Hayes grinned and patted his younger brother on the back. "You just want to visit with Julia."

Seth's ears blushed red as he smirked. "Hey, she likes me."

"Easy now." Graham's voice called from behind them and had them both tossing smirks over their shoulders.

"I'm going to be at the feed store tomorrow," Clint interrupted. "Philip said he could use some help."

Calvin eyed Graham and they both rolled their eyes. The work was hot, long, and hard for the day, and the outcome was just as they expected.

"He mentioned it," Graham said.

"In air conditioning? All day?" Hayes asked him.

"Yep." Clint grinned.

"You're going to grow soft," Hayes warned.

"Not in a day."

"We'll see about that."

"You're just jealous," Clint laughed.

"Not at all," Hayes countered. "I'm not meant to be inside all day. I have to be in the open air or I'd suffocate."

"Same here." Lawrence slipped his gloves off his hands and beat them against his pant leg. "Even if the day sucks, it's better than standing behind a counter."

"We'll see." Clint, his amused expression slowly fading at his brothers' lack of envy, grew quiet.

"This was just pulling and rolling up fence wire, Graham," Calvin spoke softly as they watched their brothers climb in their trucks and head out. When Hayes tossed the last wave, Cal raised his voice to its normal clarity. "If Clint's already bailing now, then the hopes of him actually helping to build the new fence are slim."

"It's up to him," Graham reminded him.

"I know. Just frustrates me, I guess."

Graham shrugged. "I prefer less headaches in my life. If Clint wants to work in town instead of leaving work half-finished here, I'm all for it."

Calvin sighed as he removed his hat and slid it onto the dash of his truck. "I'm headed into town now. Holler at me if you need something."

"What are you doing in town?"

"Going to pick up lug nuts for Alice's truck and then head over to her place to work on a plan to convert that house to central air and heat."

"She meeting you there?" Graham asked, his tone curious.

"Not that I know of." Calvin slid into his truck, unaware of Graham's amused expression. "See you in the morning." Graham nodded and headed towards his own house.

Calvin wanted to shower first. He felt weary in his joints and knew that a glass of icecold water and a hot shower would do him wonders, revive him for the second part of his day. But that time would have to come later. Though he may treat himself to one of Sloppy's meals if he wrapped up later than he planned. He glanced at his watch. It was past six already. By the time he got to town, he'd be lucky if the parts store was still open. He'd do his best to swing by there first before heading to Al's place.

The thought of converting Alice's house from a poorly performing window unit to central air and heat had been playing itself through his mind for a couple of weeks. The small, box-framed house would be easy to convert, he thought, without much remodel work needed on the inside. He'd see what he could draft up and then run the idea by her. He pulled into the parts store parking lot and darted up the old cement steps grooved by years of boots stomping on their surface. The old bell rang above the door and Doris stepped out from the rear storage room and converted office space. "Let me guess, you're here for the lug nuts?"

"I am." Calvin grinned. "How are you, Doris?"

"Still single." She winked at him, her wrinkled skin crinkling around the corners of her eyes and lips as she smiled. "How are you? Still bending over backwards to help that Wilkenson girl?"

"I take it Alice hasn't beat me here today, hm?"

"Nope. Haven't seen her. That girl would lose her head if it weren't anchored down."

"She has a full plate most days."

"As do you, sweetie." She tossed her finger at him in warning. "You don't let her take advantage of that sweet heart of yours, you hear?"

Calvin flushed but he shrugged. "Just helping a friend out."

"Right. Well, I will fetch the lug nuts. Hold tight." She shuffled her way to the back room and came out carrying a small paper sack. "Put it on your account?"

"Yes ma'am. I appreciate it."

"I appreciate you coming in at end of day. Seeing a handsome man perks me right up for the rest of the evenin'."

Laughing, Calvin nodded his farewell and headed out. He had a key to Alice's place from all his previous maintenance trips, so getting into the little house was easy. The sight of it uninhabited made it look sadder than it already did on the exterior. He grabbed a clipboard out of his tool chest and a pen from his dash. He took his time drafting the small house, taking measurements, and even making a new list of repairs or improvements that could be made to liven up the place. If Alice continued living on the ranch, she should sell or rent the little house out. Not only would it be some income, but it would also put someone in the place instead of it sitting empty. Empty houses didn't fare well. And he didn't like to see Alice living in such disarray. He was thankful Julia made the move to Parks and that she and Alice resided in Graham's guesthouse. It suited both women to have each other's company. Alice was less grumpy having a close friend around. And she was more organized than ever having Julia run the books and office. His phone rang.

"You beat me to the parts store?" Alice, winded from what he knew was a last-minute sprint up the steps before Doris flipped the sign, could be heard slamming the door to her truck.

"I did. I figured it'd save you a trip."

"Yeah, if you'd called and told me. I just got a scolding from Doris about having you as my man slave."

Calvin smirked at Doris's loyalty. "Sorry. I'll work on getting them on your tires this evening when I get back."

"Where are you now?"

"At your place."

"Why?"

"Taking some measurements."

"Alright..." Alice waited for more of an explanation, but his silence had her sighing. "Fine. See you at the ranch."

He slipped his phone back into his pocket, unaware of her moody sign-off as he finished off his list. He walked the short distance to Sloppy's and went straight to the bar. She beamed at him, her red lips against fair skin bold and her smile welcoming. "You look like you're on your last leg, Cal."

"I'm starting to feel that way. Was going to see about some supper to go."

"Anything in particular?"

"Whatever you put in the box."

Ruby smiled. "I think I can do that. I'll try to be quick about it so you can head home." She turned and busied herself behind the bar and then slid him a glass of sweet tea. "Here. To tide you over."

CALVIN

"You have no idea how much this is needed." Cal took a long sip and nodded his thanks as she bustled towards the kitchen door, where the promising scent of fried food worked to satisfy a small portion of his weariness.

H

Chapter Four

"So, the cow is literally flipped on its back?" Julia asked, taking a sip of her after-supper wine.

"Yep."

"And you just poke a needle in and done?"

"Well, more to it than that, but yeah."

"Interesting. And the cow's back isn't hurt?"

"Nope. Not if it's done right," Alice explained.

"LDA... I'll have to make a note of that. I've never heard of that before."

Alice slid into the empty rocker on the porch as Cal's truck pulled to a stop in front of Graham's. It was after dark, and she wondered what exactly he'd been doing at her place 'taking measurements.' Not only that, that conversation was hours ago. What had he been doing since then? Or where had he gone? Honestly, it wasn't really any of her business, but she told herself that she needed to know, so as to better understand why her truck tires weren't repaired yet. Then again, that was also a selfish thought she grappled with the last hour as she answered question after question from Julia about the day's appointments and more about the treatment of rats as pets, all of which Graham found quite amusing.

Cal stepped out of his truck, his work clothes hanging on him, the dirt and sweat from the day having settled into an extra weight that seemed to make his steps drag slightly slower than normal.

"Hey Cal," Julia greeted. She pointed to Graham's beer. "Would you like one?"

He held up a hand. "No thanks. Ruby pumped me full of sweet tea."

Alice's brow rose. "Ruby, hm?"

"Yeah, I buzzed over there to grab dinner." He pointed to the white container sitting on his dash in his truck.

"You haven't eaten supper?" Julia held a hand on her chest. "Bless your heart. What have you been doing?" She turned a hard gaze towards Graham as if he were to blame for the extra work his brother took on.

Graham held up his hands in innocence.

"Runnin' some errands." He grinned. "No need to worry over me, Julia. Got those lug nuts." He looked to Alice and held up a paper bag.

"Mind if I put 'em on in the mornin'?"

"I've got to be at the clinic by seven," Alice reported.

She watched as he weighed her words and rubbed a hand over his chin. "Alright. I'll get after it."

She hadn't seen Calvin do much with reluctance, but she saw the tiredness in his shoulders when he turned and regretted that she hadn't just acquiesced.

"I'll help you." Graham handed his beer to Julia and stood.

"Good man," Julia whispered up at him as he winked at her.

Graham trudged down the steps towards Alice's truck as Calvin pointed to the troublesome tire and the others he'd swapped the nuts out on. With the two of them, the work was quick, and Alice's truck was primed and ready for the next day.

Cal walked over to Shirley and began transferring her vet bags and gear over to her own truck again.

"You could help him," Julia whispered. "Instead of making him do it all."

"Graham's down there."

"Alice." Julia eyed her friend with disappointment. "He's exhausted."

Alice pointed towards the men walking back towards them. "And they're already done."

"I'll pick Shirley up tomorrow and move her back to my place."

"I forgot to fill her up before bringing her home." Alice admitted. "I didn't think of that until just now, but I'll have Julia cut you a check from the clinic for some gas money."

"Don't worry about it," Cal sighed. "Well, I think I'm going to finally head home, shower, and eat some supper. Call it a night."

"Thank you for seeing about the truck," Julia said, elbowing Alice.

"Right. Yes. Thanks. I appreciate you loaning me Shirley. She can really move if you want her to."

Cal smirked. "Don't mention it. Night." He pulled away before being roped into more conversation, a clear sign he was officially done for the day. And he also didn't toss out a witty comeback about her driving skills. Alice watched him leave in disappointment. Was he just tired? Or tired of her? She wasn't quite sure. Neither sat well with her.

"Well, I think I'm going to head on in as well." She pointed to the guesthouse. "It's been a long day."

"Yes. And you need your rest for tomorrow. Those rat tumors are awaiting," Julia teased.

"For your newfound fascination, I'm going to make you sit in on the consultation."

Julia's horrified face had her laughing and Graham bellowed as well, receiving a firm backhand to his chest from Julia in response. "Gotta learn sometime, Jewels." Alice grinned, her spirits slightly higher as she shuffled into the house.

∞

The brothers had plenty of time the next morning to finish pulling wire and Cal found himself where he fit best, on a machine. He loved working with machines, the standard tractor being a particular favorite of his. This particular tractor belonged to his grandpa and his dad, passed down from rancher to rancher. And thanks to his forefathers' attention to maintenance and proper care, the tractor had years left under its belt. He intended to keep it that way. Graham worked with him as he pulled fence posts from the ground. He'd use the tractor to tug up the post, and Graham would unhook and stack them to the side as they went. It was slow work, but the posts were in decent shape. Some could be used for future projects on the ranch, some for the new fence line, while some would need to be disposed of, but it was important to Graham to assess the value as they went and pinch pennies where they could. Ranching was an expensive business with some lean years of payout. It was smart to operate on a low budget as best they could. Yes, in their grandparents' day, the west Texas glory days of the oil boom did not skip the Hastings Ranch and some of that "glory money", as their father used to call it, remained stashed away for a rainy day. But the brothers did not like to dip into the family fund for trivial things if they could make the ranch stand on its own feet. And now that mineral rights were out of their hands, the oil money no longer existed as current income for them. All they had was what was left from their father, which wasn't much in the grand scheme of things. But thanks to Graham's leadership, the ranch had operated smoothly and in the positive for over a decade, though some years were better than others. Cal was thankful for the work, for the land, and for his brothers. Their situation was unique. Not all ranches could operate like they did. Not all families could work together like they did. But losing their parents brought them all closer together. Difficult decisions were made as a family, and it was together that all the brothers had decided to keep the ranch. They'd had opportunities to sell. Philip, in particular, was more open to the idea, but had since come around. Though he didn't work the ranch day to day with the rest of them, his brother provided and helped them in ways that helped save the bottom dollar, and that was just as important.

Seth and Clint were still finding their groove. Seth seemed content on the place. Clint, well, he'd blow away with the slightest breeze if he had the courage to let loose and fly. But there was hesitancy there. A young, wild heart that just hadn't found what suited him yet. Calvin understood that. Though it bugged him to see his brother slacking, he knew it would need to be Clint's decision on what he wanted out of life and where he wanted to end up. Graham seemed more patient about the prospect of Clint leaving than Cal. But they had a full staff whether Clint stayed or left and plenty of work to keep them all busy. Work they all loved.

Graham held up a hand for him to pause the tractor as he hooked the next post. Receiving the thumbs up, Cal lifted the bucket and the post was free and set aside. His phone buzzed in his pocket. Surprised that he had cell service this far out, he glanced down.

Alice: One of you boys needs to call me ASAP.

Alice, in her typical demanding way, had summoned the Hastings group text. He held up a hand to Graham to let him know he was pausing a moment. He didn't have enough service to make a call, but he quickly texted back.

Cal: What's up?

Alice: Annie needs us. NOW!

Cal: On our way.

He turned off the tractor and hopped out.

"What's going on?" Graham asked, leaning against their next post.

"Al just texted us all. Annie's got some sort of trouble."

"What kind of trouble?"

"She didn't say. Just that Annie needs us now."

"Alright. Go ahead and head that way. She need all of us?"

"I have no idea. Figure if she texted the group it meant more than one of us."

"Alright." Graham rubbed his chin. "We'll go. I want Lawrence and Seth to keep pulling wire. I'll grab Hayes to come along."

"Sounds good. I'll meet you guys in town. I'll call and let you know what's going on."

Graham nodded and hurried towards his truck to drive the mile down towards the rest of the brothers as Cal hurried towards his own and headed towards town.

Contrary to popular belief, Calvin could drive faster than the speed limit if need be, and he made it to town faster than his norm. He pulled into Annie's driveway behind Alice's work truck and hurried towards the front door. He entered without knocking. "Hey hey," he called out.

"In here!" Alice called from the den at the back of the house.

He knew Annie would have his hide for wearing his boots in the house, but the urgency in Alice's tone had him hoping for future forgiveness. He walked into the room to find Annie, angry, hands on her hips, as she stared down at the floor where her husband, Henry, sat leaning against base of the sofa. Her eyes softened when she saw Cal, the steel gaze briefly flashing to his boots before she waved him into the room.

"What happened?"

"Henry decided to try and change the lightbulb in the ceiling fan." Annie shook her head and rolled her eyes at what she obviously deemed stupidity. "He fell, and he refuses to let me call an ambulance to help him up."

Henry, his head leaning back against the sofa cushion looked up at Cal. "All I need is a strong arm to help me stand. I'll be fine. The women are frettin' over nothin.'"

Cal's lips twitched as he stepped forward. He could help Henry to his feet on his own if the man didn't look like he was in severe pain. But Henry was a round man, heavy set. Cal doubted he could make the lift and support all of Henry if the man couldn't help support himself just a little bit. He heard the front door open and Graham and Hayes hurried inside just in time.

"What happened?" Hayes's panicked gaze flashed towards Annie and her bravado weakened just a tad when he wrapped an arm around her shoulders and gave her an encouraging squeeze.

"Henry was being a fool," she said. "Again."

"Starting to make that a habit, Henry?" Hayes asked, the older man chuckling and then grimacing at the effort.

"Can you stand?" Graham asked.

"Yes. Just need a boost to the feet," Henry told him.

Cal and Graham each reached under Henry's arms and Hayes stood at the ready to intervene if they needed him. When they hoisted Henry to his feet, the older man's right leg gave out, sending him crashing into Graham's chest. Henry gasped and nodded towards the sofa. "Just set me down there."

They did, slowly. Pain washed over Henry's face. "I think it's my hip. Somethin's not right."

Cal looked to Alice and she stepped forward to assess the problem.

"I'm not a bull," Henry barked.

"Could have fooled me." Annie replied. "Let Alice take a look at you. She'll know if we need to take you to the hospital."

"Honestly, all this fuss..." Henry acquiesced to Alice's care and gasped as she placed pressure near his right hip joint.

"I think you need some x-rays, Henry. Just to make sure you didn't break anything. Could just be bruised, but we'll want to make sure."

"Just need an ice pack and some rest."

"No. The doctor has spoken." Annie snapped her fingers. "Boys, lets load him up."

Grumbling, but allowing the help, Graham and Calvin raised him to his feet again. Henry could barely place pressure on his right leg. Thankfully, Graham supported that side and was able to withstand the extra weight to get him towards Annie's car.

"Need us to follow?" Hayes asked.

"No. The doctors can help him out when we get there," Alice said. "Thanks for coming. He didn't want the fuss of an ambulance, but I knew he needed to get moving." She ran a hand through her hair and her worry matched their own.

"Let us know," Graham reminded her.

She nodded.

"You need one of us to go along with you?" Cal asked her quietly, his hand briefly brushing down her arm and to her hand. He could tell seeing Henry, their beloved Henry, in such a state had shaken her up. He could tell Annie was too, though both women were too stubborn to admit it. Alice briefly squeezed his hand before dropping it. "No, I think we'll be fine. Just don't like seeing him like this. Scared Annie to death."

"I can tell. She's meaner and madder than a hornet."

Alice's soft smirk and watery eyes had him pulling her to him in a brief hug. When she stepped back, she inhaled a deep breath and sighed. "Alright, off we go. I'll call you when I know something."

"Yeah, send a text too. We're in the back pasture and service is sketchy. I think I only got your text because I was up on the tractor."

"Will do. Thanks for coming so quickly."

Nodding, he stepped back so she could slide into Annie's car as well and they could be on their way.

The three men stood and watched as Alice drove in her usual racecar fashion towards Sheffield Hospital.

∞

"A broken hip," Henry reported with a sad shake of his head. He didn't like it. Annie didn't like it. And Alice, grateful they had an answer, didn't like it either, but knew that it was one way to teach the older man his limitations. Sometimes hard lessons were the best lessons.

"You'll have to take it easy after the surgery," Alice warned him. "No jumping, running, climbing."

He grinned. "I think I can manage that."

"And no ridiculous notions of changin' lightbulbs. That is one reason we have seven boys, Henry. They're to take care of those tasks."

"They're busy workin', Annie. A lightbulb is no reason for a special trip to town."

"You're a special reason," Alice stated. "Both of you are. And the brothers don't mind coming into town. Nor do I or Julia. We can change a lightbulb just as easily as the men can."

Annie rubbed a hand over her back. "That's right. We are surrounded by a brood of youngins',

Henry. Now, the doctor said we needed to reevaluate your diet."

"Oh, Lord." Henry leaned back against the hospital bed pillow.

"No groaning. We knew the day was coming when you couldn't smother things in butter and bacon grease and expect to stay slim."

Alice, knowing 'slim' was not a word she'd use to describe Henry, bit back a grin as he pretended to be disgusted at the thought of a diet. Truth was, Henry would do anything for Annie, even give up his sweet tooth or butter consumption.

"Limited red meats," Annie continued, and Henry opened his mouth to debate, but she quickly silenced him with one of her famous glares. "Now, rest. Alice and I are going to step out to grab a coffee." Annie pulled Alice out into the hallway and closed the door. "You need to get back to work."

"I don't mind staying. Dad said he could cover the clinic as long as necessary."

"We are fine here now, Alice. I thank you for coming to our aid and calling the boys."

"I'm glad I was in the area when you called. You going to be okay?"

Annie's face softened. "Yes, sweetie, I am. We'll have to make a few adjustments over the next few weeks and months, but it's nothing Henry and I can't handle."

"You're two of the strongest people I know," Alice admitted.

"And don't you forget it." Annie smiled. "And I want you and Julia to treat those boys, *all* the boys, to a lovely dinner on our behalf. In thanks."

"They don't mind helping either."

"I know it, but Calvin looked like poor skin and bones. Hayes looked worn out. And if it weren't for Julia, Graham would be looking the same as his brothers. I haven't been out there to check on them, so I'm asking you girls to do it for me. Make sure they're eatin' right and makin' time to take care of themselves in the midst of the summer heat."

"Part of Calvin's problem is me," Alice explained. "I've been keeping him busy."

"Oh?" Annie's brow rose. "With what?"

"My lack of personal responsibility."

Annie fisted her hands on her hips. "That truck again?"

"Yes. Though it was not my fault this time. And apparently he's doing something at my house. Or wants to and has been making drafts of some sort."

"Probably wants to help you make it livable. That Cal is a sweetheart, Alice Wilkenson. If you don't want him investing his time and energy in your house or you, you better tell him right up front. He's always had a soft spot for ya. Now if you take advantage of that, I'll whoop you to high heaven and then down to Hades himself. Otherwise, Cal will wear himself out tryin' to take care of ya."

"My house is fine. I keep telling him that."

"Your house is a death trap, honey. And it looks like a rejected doll house."

"Well, tell me how you really feel, Annie," Alice chuckled.

"I am. And again, if you want help with it, you treat that boy with kindness and see about him in return. Otherwise, sell it and be done with it."

"I know you're right. I just haven't really had time to worry about it."

"Well, now you do." Annie smiled. "Because I'm going to keep bugging you about it."

"I believe you will."

"I'm a woman of my word." Annie held up her finger in oath. "Now, get. Go on now. Get to work. I'll update the lot of you if anything changes."

Alice hugged the petite woman close and breathed in her familiar scent, one more comfortable and welcoming than her own mother's. Annie had always been her second mom. Her birth mother, Wanda—Alice cringed at the name—did her duty until Alice was around four years old. Realizing Parks and family life weren't for her, Wanda took off, and other than a few phone calls throughout the years, created the life she always wanted somewhere in Vegas. Her father had never remarried, and Alice never questioned his choice. It was the two of them. And with the help of Annie and Henry and the Hastings brothers, they'd all become their own mixed and matched family. A family she cherished and counted herself fortunate to have.

She eyed her watch and dialed Julia on her way out of the hospital. Giving a quick update on Henry, she then pitched the idea of closing the clinic early if possible and making dinner for the brothers. Julia loved cooking for people, so it didn't take much convincing.

"I'll stop and grab what we need on the way home. Your dad said he'd finish up the last handful of patients and close the clinic so I can be on the way," Julia explained.

"Tell him thanks for filling in today."

"I will, though I don't think it's required. He has had a blast today. I think he's missed it."

"I knew he would."

"Well, I'll see you in a bit." Julia hung up and Alice dragged herself out to her truck and decided to make a pit stop at her place in Parks. She hadn't been to the little house in weeks since Julia moved out to the ranch. She hadn't a reason to now that she lived in Graham's guesthouse. But it was time to check on things. Though she knew Calvin would have given the place a thorough comb over, she wanted to view the place as unattached as possible, look for potential or look for the improvements that everyone else seemed to notice. And if she were honest with herself, she just needed a few minutes of quiet time to herself, and her little house seemed like an oasis at the moment. Turning towards Parks, she zoned out on the familiar drive, and before she knew it, sat in front of her small-framed house.

H

Chapter Five

"*Call it a day!*" Graham's voice called over the rumbling maintainer's motor. Cal waved him on. He just wanted to finish smoothing out the dirt where he and Graham had pulled up posts, and then he'd call it quits. After Henry's debacle, he and Graham were able to finish up the remaining posts thanks to Seth and Lawrence wrapping up the rest of pulling wire and staples. It was a productive day from all of them. Now he wished to smooth out the path so that they could lay out the new posts the following day or day after if Philip's order arrived by then. Graham tapped a hand to the side of the machine and signaled to cut the engine. Cal, annoyed he couldn't get a bit ahead, turned the machine off. "Alice and Julia want us at the house for supper. All of us."

"Give me a half hour to finish this hundred-yard stretch."

Graham shook his head. "Call it a day, Cal. Seriously."

Calvin sighed. "Fine. I gotcha." He hopped out of the machine. "Was just trying to get ahead."

"I'm all for it, but Annie gave Alice orders to feed us all."

"Alice?"

"Well, Julia... via Alice," Graham smirked.

"Now that sounds like a promising supper."

"Agreed."

"I'll head up after a shower."

"Good. The other guys are already headed that way."

"I'm sure they are. No one is going to turn down Julia's cookin'."

Graham's rare smile flashed quickly in pride as he headed towards his truck. He tossed a wave as Calvin headed towards his own house. When he pulled up, Alice sat on his front steps. Curious as to why she'd be hanging at his place, he eased out of the truck, the door creaking as he closed it behind it. "Al, to what do I owe the pleasure."

"Oh, I was just 'taking measurements.'" She stood and dusted off her backside as he walked forward.

"Mmhmm. Measurements for what?"

"You tell me. I went by my place today. So what has you so interested over there?"

"Ah. Mind if I get my shower first and then we can ride over to Graham's and I'll tell you?"

"I have to go help Julia food prep."

"Then go. I'll see you over there. We can talk about your house later."

"I want to know now." She fisted her hands on her hips. "What's wrong with my house?"

"Several things, actually. The porch is sagging, there's rot along the roofline, there's the screen door that needs to be replaced, the AC unit needs replaced... still."

"Well, I'm not living there right now, so I don't see a huge rush in fixing everything."

"I'm not saying you have to. I just think it needs to be done so you can decide what to do with the place. Rent it, sell it... up to you. But it needs a bit of care."

"And you think I need you to do that for me?"

"No. I just thought it would be a nice gesture to make a list for you and let you decide what you want to do."

Irritated, she huffed and her bangs danced along her forehead.

"Just trying to help, Al."

"I know. But I don't need it."

"Okay. Fine. I'll stop. I didn't realize it was that big of deal to you."

"It's not."

"Obviously it is if you're waiting on my front porch to lash out at me about it."

"I'm not lashing out."

He tilted his head in disbelief. "What brought this on?"

"What do you mean?"

"I've always helped you with the house or your truck. You've never minded. Why does it bother you now?"

"It doesn't bother me."

"Liar," he smirked.

"Fine," she huffed. "Annie made a comment that I take advantage of your kindness."

"Ah. I see." He shuffled towards his front door. "Feeling guilty, hm?"

"Not guilty, just… well, I'd much rather you ask me before just jumping into something on my behalf."

"Alright. I'll do that then. Now, can I go shower?"

Alice studied him a moment. He could tell she had more on her mind, but a ding to her cell phone told her Julia was summoning her to Graham's to help with supper. "I'll let it be for now," she told him.

He shrugged on his way into his house. "See ya in a bit." He heard her truck head towards the main house and thought it interesting that she didn't want his help all of a sudden, with her house or anything. No telling what Annie had said, but typically it never mattered to Alice what people thought. That was new. And curious.

He made quick work of showering, his stomach rumbling for what he knew would be a delicious feast provided by the beautiful Julia. He still hadn't quite figured out how she and Alice were such close friends. They were polar opposites in almost every aspect. Though, if he admitted it, both were beautiful, just in their own way. But the rest of their lives and personalities were as different as night and day. As Julia grew more comfortable with his family, he hoped to one day find out how she'd connected with Alice in college other than being roommates.

He pulled in front of Graham's house and accepted the cold beer Lawrence handed him on his way up the steps. "We've been confined to the steps," his brother reported.

"I see." Cal walked inside anyway to give his thanks to Julia. He was surprised to find Alice standing at the stove stirring something in a large pot. Her hair, down around her shoulders just a few minutes ago at his house, was now pulled back into a sloppy bun on top of her head as her firm concentration was on the pot and stirring. "Well, this is a sight."

Julia glanced up from the island and her chopping of lettuce and smiled. "Hey, Cal. Glad you made it. Graham said he had to pull a few teeth to get you to stop working today."

"Teeth intact." He grinned. "I wouldn't stop for anything less than your cookin'."

She beamed and accepted the small side hug from him as he nodded towards Alice. "I'm impressed you've got her at the stove."

"I can hear you," Alice tossed over her shoulder.

Calvin walked over and peered into the pot and then to her. His eyes studied her profile, the cute furrow on her forehead, the hair up that he'd hardly ever seen over the years, and the light trace of flour on her cheek that was almost, if not a little more appealing than the contents of the pot she stirred. "Smells good," he said, his eyes not leaving her face.

She caught his stare and her cheeks flushed. He'd never complimented her in such bold fashion, but something about her at the stove, insecure but trying hard, twisted something in his belly.

"Yeah, well, it's going to be delicious," Alice stated with confidence.

"I have no doubt about it." He lightly dusted the flour off her cheek and she jolted, the whisk dropping from her fingers into the pot.

"Shoot!" Alice tried to fish it out and hissed as her fingers slightly scorched under the heat. Cal reached in and retrieved it. "Stop distracting me."

"Wasn't my intention."

"Well, you are. Now go outside with the rest of your brothers."

"There you are, bossy," Cal whispered, nudging her with his elbow.

Alice held his gaze a moment. Steam rose from the pot as something shifted in the air between them. He ducked his head and backed away, curious as to what he felt, but also a bit nervous as well. He turned to find Julia smiling behind their backs. She diverted her gaze back to her salad prepping so as not to embarrass him, for which he was thankful. Retrieving his opened beer from the counter on his way out, he slipped out the screen door and onto the porch.

∞

"Phew!" Julia chuckled. "That was intense over there. How you doing?"

Alice narrowed her eyes at her friend. "Don't start."

Julia giggled. "What? I'm just recovering from all the heat in this room." She fanned herself and then laughed again as Alice bit back a smirk. "Seriously though... something's different there."

"Yeah, well, I don't know what it is, so I'd rather not talk about it."

"Why not?" Julia looked baffled. "It's just you and me in here."

"And a whole gaggle of Hastings brothers on the porch who have expert eavesdropping skills. Help me hash it out later."

"Oh, I will definitely want to help."

Shaking her head, Alice turned back to the gravy. "I think I actually succeeded this time. Thick and creamy."

Julia walked over and peered into the pot. "Looks good." She raised the whisk and swiped some of the white gravy onto her finger and tasted.

Nodding, she added a couple of pinches of salt and pepper. "I think that should do it. I'll call the guys in."

She walked to the door and the men filtered into the house and settled at the long, wooden dining table scarred by years of use. Generations of use. Each sat into their chairs they'd occupied over the years. "What's on the menu?" Seth asked as he scooted closer to the table. Julia placed a plate in front of him that housed a large chicken fried steak, a huge dollop of mashed potatoes, and a stack of buttery green beans. He gave a low whistle of appreciation as Julia placed another plate in front of Hayes. Alice fetched Lawrence and Calvin a plate and set them down in front of them.

She then walked over to the island and Julia handed her the salad bowl to take to the table while she carried the gravy and a basket of homemade rolls.

"You ladies out did yourselves." Lawrence placed a roll onto his plate as he passed the basket to Calvin.

"Well, Annie insisted." Julia gently laid her hand on Graham's shoulder, his hand sliding up to hold it there as she waited for him to say the blessing over their food. When he finished, she topped off their glasses of tea before finding her seat. Alice, squeezed between Hayes and Seth, took a bite of her own steak and had to admit her gravy did turn out rather awesome.

"How's Henry? Do we have an update?" Graham asked.

Alice sliced through her steak. "Just that he's ready to go home. However, his surgery is scheduled for tomorrow morning around ten."

"We can make that." Graham nodded towards all his brothers and they nodded in agreement.

"Good. Annie's hanging in there, but I can tell this has shaken her," Alice explained.

"He definitely didn't look good when we went by to help today," Calvin added.

"Well, maybe this will wake both of them up to the fact they are not invincible, and they'll slow down a bit," Hayes said hopefully.

"Impossible." Seth shook his head as the sound of a truck could be heard pulling up to the house. Graham turned and then nodded to Julia. She stood and welcomed Clint with a warm smile. "Come on in, we just sat down. I'll bring you a plate."

Clint walked to the sink and washed his hands before claiming his usual seat at the table.

"How was town today?" Hayes asked.

"Good. Not too bad. Different."

"That's it?" Lawrence asked. "That's all you're going to tell us?"

Clint shrugged. "What is there to tell?"

"Did you like it?" Seth asked.

Another shrug.

Cal shot a glance towards Graham.

"Will you be helping Philip out tomorrow?" Graham asked.

"I think so. Unless you need me here."

Graham shook his head and took a bite of steak and Alice could have sworn she saw a brief wave of disappointment flash across Clint's face at not being missed for the day. She wondered what he was trying to prove or pull off by working in town versus on the ranch. She caught Calvin's perceptive eye and sent him a mental inquiry. He just shook his head in a "not now, tell you later" fashion.

"Tomorrow we will pause on the fence project so we can go be with Annie during Henry's surgery. After that, Cal's got a lineup of maintenance to do, so if you need an oil change or anything, tell him today so he can grab supplies in town." Graham took the light tap to his arm from Julia as a warning and stopped talking about work. Alice bit back a smirk as she saw how hard it was for Graham to keep quiet and not boss his brothers around.

"I've got to swing by Doc Wilkenson's tomorrow." Hayes nodded towards Alice. "Your dad called me today about one of your patients wanting to sell a horse for cheap."

"Who?" Alice asked.

"Tim Sampson, I think it was," Hayes said. "I don't know him, but I'm all about checking out a horse."

"Ah. Tim. He rescues abused horses, rehabilitates them, and then sells them. Or at least that was his intentions several years ago. I don't think it's quite worked out the way he planned in terms of business. Turns out people don't really want an emotionally unstable horse."

"I imagine not. It's hard for a horse to adjust to new people or even other horses after a life like that. Much like people." The sympathy on Hayes's face sobered everyone.

"Just be sensible," Graham reminded him. Everyone knew Hayes had a soft spot for horses, much less those in need of a better life.

"And be wary of Tim Sampson," Alice added.

"Is he not trustworthy?" Hayes asked.

She shrugged. "All I know is that he receives a lot of horses and so far, none have been fully rehabilitated. So he's either terrible at what he claims to do, or he doesn't even try. Have me or my dad thoroughly check the horse out if you intend to buy it."

Hayes nodded in agreement as he popped an overly large bite of mashed potatoes in his mouth, Julia smiling like a proud parent at her food being so enjoyed.

"Dad will cover the office again tomorrow so we can be with Annie," Alice told Julia. "Let's plan on riding with Graham."

Graham looked up from his plate. "Sure."

"I wasn't asking."

"I'm aware," he returned with a narrowed gaze.

"Oh, don't act like it's an inconvenience. You know you planned to sweep Julia away so the two of you could ride together. What's one more?" She pointed to herself.

"Ride with Cal." Graham nodded to his brother.

"*Or*," Julia interrupted. "we could all be adults and just all ride together. No sense in everyone taking their own vehicles."

"Everyone has different errands to run," Graham explained.

"So? Can we not wait five minutes while Cal runs in the auto parts store to grab what he needs?"

Calvin, silent through the exchange, was surprised they even cared whether or not he drove his own vehicle. He looked to Alice and she rolled her eyes on a shrug as though she had no idea why Julia wished for them to all ride together. But Alice definitely knew. Her friend's match-making wheels were turning, something Alice had to put a stop to soon. Tonight. Otherwise, she'd be dressed in white and saying 'I do' before she could blink.

H

Chapter Six

Pacing wasn't in his nature. In general, Calvin kept a level head in most situations and was able to support or calm others who struggle with panic. Like Alice. When Alice was stressed, worried, or hurt, she was like a fuse just waiting to blow. He watched her circle the enclosed waiting room of the hospital, Julia trying to settle her friend's nerves to no avail.

"Shouldn't we have heard something by now?" Alice asked. "I mean, how long does this take?"

"It is a hip replacement," Clint reiterated. "I'm sure it takes a few hours, Al."

Annie walked into the waiting room carrying a fresh cup of coffee, her face downcast until she saw everyone waiting for her. "Well, isn't this nice." She accepted a firm hug from Seth and then made her rounds. "You kids didn't have to come all this way."

Philip stepped back from his hug and kissed her cheek. "We wouldn't miss being here for you or Henry for anything." She patted his cheek before embracing Cal. "Well, you sure do know how to make an old lady feel loved. Henry will feel so blessed knowing you all turned up."

"So how much longer?" Alice asked.

"They just took him into surgery about fifteen minutes ago. There's time yet," Annie sighed.

"Have you eaten?" Graham asked her.

"Oh, fiddle faddle! I'm fine. I've got coffee and my family, I don't need food just yet."

Graham sent a look towards Julia and she nodded at the silent task of making sure Annie kept her strength up throughout the day.

Annie sat in a chair and patted the one next to her for Alice. "I heard you've been making the rounds quite well the last couple weeks. Your daddy is so proud of you."

Alice flushed under the praise. "Only because I have Julia to hold down the clinic."

"That is true," Annie acknowledged. "I also heard you were seen driving Cal's Shirley through town." Annie raised a curious brow.

Alice's lack of enthusiasm disappointed Annie. "Yes, well, apparently my truck was having some issues, so Cal insisted. I'm sure the rumor mill is abuzz."

"And that he was seen at your little house in town."

"He won't stay away." Alice shrugged. "He wants to fix things. He can't help himself."

Annie chuckled.

"I knew people would get the wrong idea. Just thought I had a bit more time before that happened."

"Oh, honey, it could be worse." Annie nodded towards Seth as he sat with his head leaned back against the wall, mouth ajar, and an unattractive snore spouted out. They both laughed.

"I guess you're right."

"I keep telling her it's not a bad idea at all," Julia whispered, sliding a chair closer to be a part of the conversation.

Annie bit back a laugh at Alice's horrified expression.

"Don't look at me that way." Julia held up an accusatory finger. "Do you remember last night in the kitchen?"

"What happened in the kitchen?" Annie turned towards Alice in expectation.

"Nothing."

"It wasn't nothing," Julia assured Annie. "Definitely some tension between the two. *Good* tension," Julia reiterated.

"Oh?" Annie asked, looking to Alice again.

"We are not talking about this here." Alice crossed her arms and leaned back in her chair.

"Now, Alice Wilkenson, I need a distraction. You wouldn't deny me an intriguing conversation while my husband—my dear, dear, dear Henry—is in surgery, would you?" Annie batted her lashes and Alice rolled her eyes. Julia grinned.

"Fine. Cal's been intrusive. Pushy. Everywhere. And weird. There. Happy?"

"Not really." Calvin's voice had Alice jolting in her seat as the women turned to see him standing holding three cups of coffee in his hands. He handed one to Julia and then offered one to Alice, that she reluctantly accepted, avoiding his gaze. He wasn't sure what the women had been discussing, but he'd never thought his help towards Alice was seen as pushy. He didn't mean to make her feel like he was all in her business. In fact, he'd enjoyed their most recent interactions. But it seemed that was all one-sided. He caught a brief glimpse of sympathy from Julia as she thanked him for the coffee. He silently made his way back towards his brothers and slipped his hand in his pocket as he listened to Philip and Clint discuss the feed store and 'areas of opportunity' for Clint to improve upon.

"People are cheap," Clint said. "You give them the price and every single one of them wants to try and barter with you. No. Price is what it says. I don't have time to negotiate with every single person."

Philip shrugged. "Ranching isn't cheap. They want to make sure they can get the best deal. We do the same thing."

"Still. It's annoying."

"That may be, but we don't treat them like they're annoying in the process or we lose customers."

"I take it Clint won't be your new customer service manager?" Calvin asked.

Both Clint and Philip shook their heads.

"Not for a while," Philip chuckled. "Just takes some getting used to."

"We'll see how it goes this week. But right now, I'm not sure why you ever left the ranch." Clint looked to Philip for an answer and his brother just sipped his coffee.

Cal was surprised to hear Clint's lack of enthusiasm, especially considering he'd reported that things were fine to Hayes at dinner the night before. "We could say the same for you," Cal interjected.

"I need space," Clint stated. "Graham is too controlling. You can't take a breath without him counting the seconds. And if you're off by what he considers the right number, you never hear the end of it. I needed a break. He doesn't listen to ideas either."

Cal wasn't sure what the last comment was about, but he made a note to talk to Graham to see. If Graham's bossing was the only thing bothering Clint, then that could easily be settled. Graham could be overbearing. It was his nature. Big brother Graham took his role seriously and if he knew that was the only problem Clint had, he may tone down his authoritarian approach with the brother and everyone would be happy.

∞

Henry was settled. Surgery was successful. Annie was at his bedside, and all who'd gathered over the last few hours were dispersing. Alice pointed towards Seth's truck and Julia waved from Graham's. The ride to the hospital had been a quiet one. Julia and Graham in the front seat, Calvin and

Alice in the back, just as Julia planned. However, her friend's designs to engage Alice and Calvin failed. They mostly argued, as per their norm. The grass was too dry. No, it was too green. The road was bumpy and needed attention. No, it was just weathered. The sky is blue. No, it's more of an icy blue. It didn't matter the topic, she and Cal were going to disagree. She wasn't up for that kind of ride again, so she forced Seth to take her along with him. What she'd forgotten about Seth, however, is that he is a chatterbox, so as she listened to him discuss the Masons' daughter for a half hour. She felt elated when the ranch entrance came into view. All she wanted was to change clothes, curl up in front of the television and veg out the rest of the day. If she was going to have the rest of the day off, then she'd enjoy it to the fullest. Hopping out of Seth's truck, she waved in thanks.

"Hey," Julia greeted when she walked in. "I was going to change and do some yoga if you want to join."

"No thanks." Alice grinned. "I'm going to watch tv."

"You could do yoga *while* watching tv," Julia suggested.

"Where's the fun in that?"

Julia smirked. "Okay then, mind if I do yoga while you watch tv then? I don't want to lock myself in the room."

Indifferent, Alice shrugged. "I'm fine with that. Just don't block my view of the hunky hero."

Laughing, Julia walked to her room to change clothes. "Oh," she called over her shoulder, "did you apologize to Calvin?"

"For what?" Alice fished around in the cabinet for a glass and filled it to the brim with cold sweet tea.

"For what he overheard at the hospital." Julia walked back into the room wearing tights and a tank top, her hair twisted into a tight bun on top of her head.

"No. Why should I?"

"Well, your words were a bit harsh and he's helped you so much lately. Just thought it might have hurt his feelings."

"I doubt it. He's got thick skin. Plus, he needs to know when to back off."

Julia muttered something under her breath as she walked towards the living room and spread out her yoga mat. She began her exercise routine with stretches.

"Look, I've known Cal a long time," Alice explained. "If I felt like I hurt his feelings, I'd deal with it. But he's fine. Trust me. Plus, maybe he'll leave me alone about my house."

"Is it wrong of him to want to help you? I mean, you yourself were debating on what to do with the place. If he helps you fix it up, then you'd at least have some options."

"True. But then we'd have to work together. And Cal and I would not work well together. He's too... finicky."

"And you're too apathetic at times."

"Not apathetic, I just don't stress over details. I'm also busy. I don't have time to look over paint colors and tile samples."

"I don't think he planned on going that far. I think it was more 'Let's fix the giant hole in the door'," Julia defended.

"It is fixed."

"Graham's duct tape is not a fix," Julia chuckled as she went into a downward dog pose. "Oh, and Cal is working on vehicles today, so if you need an oil change, better take your truck down there at some point."

"My truck is fine."

"You sure?"

Alice caught Julia's upside-down expression and raised her shoulders. "I'm sure it is."

Groaning, Julia slipped into a different position. "Well, Graham took my car down a few minutes ago. I'm not going to turn down a free oil change."

"Let me go check my sticker." Alice trudged outside to her truck and sure enough, she was a few miles short of needing to have an updated oil change. Aggravated that her afternoon of laziness would be interrupted, she walked back into the house to grab her keys. "I'll be back in a few." Julia waved from some contortioned position as she left.

He'd been busy. Hayes had both of his trucks parked by the barn, and Seth's was lined up behind. Graham's was Cal's current project and she saw his stained denim legs protruding from underneath, no doubt emptying the oil pan. Country music blared from the old stereo he'd had since high school, the term 'boom box' plastered across the front in a tearing neon sticker that boasted he was a child of the 80s. It rested on a shelf he'd built with scrap materials from one of his handyman projects of years past. Calvin salvaged, scrapped, and created what he could from anything leftover, yet, for him to be such a scrapper, his barn was organized, tidy, and neat. He was particular about his tools and equipment. Much of the machinery on the ranch would have died slow and painful deaths if it weren't for his attention. And Alice knew that his work and skill saved the ranch valuable amounts of money.

She cleared her throat, but he didn't hear her. She then nudged one of his dirty boots with her tennis shoe.

He slowly slid out from under the truck, wiping his greasy hands on a blue towel. She pointed towards his stereo and he nodded. She walked over and turned it down as he stood and brushed off his pants. "What can I do for you, Al?"

"I need to add my truck to your list of clients today." She motioned over her shoulder. "Seems I'm a few miles short of needing an oil change."

"Let me make sure I have the supplies. Everyone else told me yesterday so I could grab everything while we were in town today."

"Well, I didn't know I needed one yesterday."

"I told everyone to check."

"Well, I didn't."

"No surprise there." Cal walked over to his shelves and began rummaging through filters and bottles.

"Besides, it's not that big of a purchase."

"It's not the purchasing that's the problem. You know every machine has their own specific requirements."

"Well, yeah, but still. If it's going to be too much trouble, I'll just take it to Jepson's tomorrow on my way to work."

"Jepson's?" Offended, Calvin turned in disgust. "Yeah, well then you'll be paying for more than an oil change, because he'll break something or put in the wrong filter which will cause problems down the road." He pulled a couple of bottles and a box. "I've got what we need here."

The boxes looked brand new, as did the oil. She knew he'd gone ahead and bought supplies for her truck while he was in town because he innately knew she'd come looking for his help. It aggravated her. She fisted her hands on her hips. "How convenient."

"Yeah. Good thing." He set them on one of his worktables. "It will be awhile. I've got a line out there. But I'll get it done."

"It's whenever. I'm home the rest of the day." She saw him chug the last of a bottle of water. He wore a greasy denim shirt, jeans with worn holes in the knees, and his boots. He looked the part of rogue ruffian and not humble rancher. Calvin rarely had facial hair. He kept a close shave. But today, stubble graced his chin and cheeks and collected the same grease and dirt from the floor. She wasn't sure why she found him so attractive this way, but the thought made her even more annoyed at him.

"Well, I'll see you."

"You're welcome," he called after her as he turned to face Graham's truck.

She grunted and then turned back around, hands on hips. "Right, I forgot. I'm supposed to shower you with words of thanks and praise for helping me out."

"What?" His brow furrowed as he rested his hands on his own hips.

"You. You're always up in my business... fixing my things, planning to repair my things or whatever, and I'm the one who is supposed to just applaud your sweet help when I didn't even ask for it in the first place."

"I didn't realize my presence or help was such an annoyance to you. I just want to help you out when I can."

"That's just it," Alice fumed. "Why? Why do you want to help me? I didn't ask you to and I don't need you to."

He nodded, brushing his palm over his chin as he let her words sink in. "Okay."

"Okay. Okay? That's it?"

He sighed. "What do you want me to say, Alice? I thought I was being a good friend by helping you. I didn't realize it rubbed you the wrong way. And if you want me to stop, I will. Simple as that."

"Okay," She said again. "Good. Thank you." She straightened her shirt before turning on her heel to leave. She realized then she had no vehicle because he was to change the oil. Did she leave it? Take it? Walk home? Needing the oil change but also realizing she'd thrown away her chances of just waiting around for it, she started walking the mile towards the guest house. If anything, maybe it would help cool her temper. He was so calm about it all. How could he not see how his actions looked? They made her look like she didn't have her life together. They also made everyone think he catered to her out of more than just friendship. What made her even more upset was that he was one of her closest friends, only now things were weird. Why did she make things weird? Frustrated, she kicked a rock out of her path. Julia. Julia is the one who'd been hinting at the fact there was more than friendship between Cal and herself. Julia had made things weird, not her. Well, Julia McComas would get an earful today as well. Alice was on a winning streak in putting people in their place, she might as well finish the job by warning her friend to mind her own business.

ℋ

Chapter Seven

"I'll give you a hundred bucks," Lawrence teased. "Just to see you do it."

"No thanks." Cal hoisted himself into the maintainer.

"Oh, come on, Cal. It'd be funny," Lawrence baited. "I'd give anything to see Al go speechless."

"Then you do it." Calvin adjusted the seat and turned on the machine. Now that they'd removed all the old fence posts, he was making a final pass with the maintainer and blade to smooth out the dirt before the new posts would be driven in with the skid steer. Meanwhile, new cedar posts were ordered from Philip, and Lawrence, if he'd decide to stop bugging Cal, was to help Hayes and Graham cut some of the old steel pipes leftover from the ranch's oil days to become new brace posts for the fence line. The goal was that by the beginning of next week they could start driving the new posts into the ground.

"Al would shoot me down," Lawrence grinned. "but I'd bet she'd say yes to you. Y'all have always been close."

"Not looking for romance, Law. Now get moving or I'll flatten ya." To drive his threat home, Calvin slipped the maintainer into gear and made his slow progression forward. Lawrence shook his head in disappointment, but he made his way towards Hayes and Graham, both with welding masks covering their faces as they worked slicing through the steel pipes. Lawrence slipped on his work gloves and began stacking the pipes they'd already trimmed, and together, the brothers worked in companionable silence.

Cal, usually content with the quiet or hum of a machine beneath him, found he wasn't able to drown out the loud thoughts in his head over Alice's tantrum the day before. He hadn't meant to make it seem like he had special intentions towards her. He just wanted to help. It's what he did. If Annie needed her house repaired, he'd do it, no questions asked. If Julia needed it, he'd do it. There was nothing special about Alice's situation. Was there? He tried to gauge his feelings on the matter. He hated gauging his feelings. Feelings usually complicated things.

He'd admit that he'd always found Alice cute. She was short and petite with pretty blonde hair. She had a great smile, the kind that ignited a person's eyes when they got excited over something. It brought light to her face and those around her. She was a firecracker. You never knew if Alice was going to hug you or punch you, and since childhood, he'd experienced both from her. And he'd admit she looked rather attractive in the kitchen with Julia the other day, her hair up and pulled away from her face. He rarely saw her like that. But other than that, he didn't seem to feel too awful much towards her except what he always had. She was his friend. A good friend. And he liked her in that department. He didn't really want to change that up. But was there something he was missing? If others thought they'd do well together, was he just not seeing past the friendship? He'd think on it some more. He wasn't one to just jump head-first into relationships. Over the years he'd only dated a handful of women, and only one he could term 'serious.' Would he like to find someone special? Sure. He'd always envisioned himself marrying and raising a family on the ranch, but it just wasn't something that occupied too much thought in his mind. He had work to do. And work was easier than dating. So much easier. Dating took time and effort that, most days, if he were honest, he didn't want to give because he was so tired from work. He looked up as Philip and Clint arrived with truck and trailer, the new cedar posts stacked neatly on the back. Philip stepped out of the truck, hands on hips as he surveyed their work. Cal tossed him a wave as he continued working. Graham would see to the new posts. He cringed when he saw Graham point Hayes in the direction of the trailer. Hayes was terrible on machines, and if he chose to unload using the skid steer, Calvin might just intervene. It wasn't that Hayes didn't know what he was doing when on a machine, he just had the most rotten luck. No machine was safe with Hayes behind the gears. Horses, on the other hand, his brother could handle with finesse.

Clint walked over to help with the unloading process as Philip and Graham bent their heads in the same fashion looking over Philip's clipboard. Philip was an asset to the ranch. Though he didn't work the land with his hands, he helped them in valuable ways. The truth about Philip was that he just wasn't cut out for life on the ranch. Now, he could handle the work, but Philip was always the social one, before Clint and Seth came along. He always wanted to "go to town" or he'd try to drag out every Sunday as long as possible so as to enjoy that break from ranch work and make the most of his time around other people besides his brothers. Henry and Annie had helped guide him towards the feed store idea. Philip had the smarts to run any business he wanted, so for him to choose the feed store was purely out of family loyalty and dedication. He'd had opportunities to leave Parks and work in the oil industry for more pay and more adventure, but he'd chosen to stay. Calvin respected him for that.

Graham held up a hand for Cal to kill the engine and he and Philip walked over. "What's up?" Cal asked.

"How much longer do you think it will take you to smooth out the rest of the fence line?" Graham asked.

"I could probably finish late this evening if I pushed it."

Graham nodded and rubbed his chin. "Phil says the rest of the posts won't be in until tomorrow afternoon."

"Okay. So, you want me to go slow or fast?"

Philip chuckled.

Graham looked up and down the fence line. "We still have to build the braces before we can drive poles into the ground." His silence meant he was mapping and reconfiguring his plan for the next day or two. Cal and Philip waited patiently. "I guess go ahead and finish up today. Tomorrow we'll build braces, and by the time the poles come in we'll have a head start and may be able to start driving poles before end of day. You good with that?" Graham asked.

Calvin nodded. "Yep. I'll be sure to eat a big lunch to last me 'til this evenin'."

Graham patted a hand against the maintainer and he and Philip walked back towards Philip's truck. Not at all annoyed that he'd have to work later than normal, Cal shifted into gear and continued smoothing the ground along the fence line.

∞

"That's eleven dogs, seven cats, a horse, a pig, and a goat. Not bad for a morning." Julia grinned at Alice as she slipped a chart back into the filing cabinet. "You've been a busy bee."

"Well, Dad's helped." Alice relaxed as she sat in an empty chair in the equally empty waiting room. "I'm starving."

"Yeah, I could definitely go for some lunch. Want to grab a sandwich?"

"If you say you packed us lunches again, I'm going to die a slow and agonizing death."

"What's wrong with my sandwiches?" Offended, Julia looked surprised to hear such disdain from her friend.

"Absolutely nothing is wrong with your sandwiches. I just want to get out of this place. I don't want to eat in the breakroom. I want to breathe some fresh air."

"Oh." Julia's frown turned into a beaming smile. "I was thinking the same thing. I did not pack lunches today, thank you very much."

"Good. Let's do it."

"What about your dad?"

"He'll go home for lunch and have his peanut butter and banana sandwich. He always does. There's no changing his routine."

Julia grabbed her purse. "We can walk too, if you want."

"Sounds good to me." Alice stepped outside and drew in a deep breath. The sun, slightly shadowed by a few rogue clouds in the bright sky, relieved some of the heat that would normally scorch the sidewalks. Yet, she still dreamed of an ice-cold soda and club sandwich. Her wish was mere seconds from being granted as she gripped the door handle of the small deli up the street from her clinic.

"Hey, Doc." Her hand froze and she looked up to see Clint Hastings walking towards her. "Julia," he greeted. "You two ladies on lunch break?"

"We are." Alice eyed him suspiciously. "What are you doing here?"

"Had to swing by the western store and pick up several orders for everybody and then some parts."

"I'm surprised Cal isn't the one picking up parts." Alice opened the door and Clint, inviting himself to lunch, grabbed the door and held it open for the women and followed them inside. "And I thought you'd be helping Philip at the feed store." Alice noted.

"I am. But Graham called and wanted the stuff picked up. We were slow at the store, and to be honest, I was bored out of my mind. So, I volunteered to drive to Sheffield."

"If you're bored at the store, then you could always go help build the fence line." Alice raised her brow, curious to see how he responded.

"They don't need me to help with that."

"Help is always needed." Julia smiled behind the words.

Clint shrugged and pasted a charming smile on his face as the cute waitress walked up to their booth to take their order.

"Seriously, Clint, what's going on with you?" Alice asked, in the way only she could. The brothers listened to her, whether they wanted to or not. She'd always had a way with them, and she'd always had a way of being heard.

"Nothing." His slumped shoulders and avoided eye contact told her quite the opposite.

"Riiiiight," Alice and Julia said in unison and crossed their arms over their chests avoiding their food as they both stared at him with narrowed gazes.

He smirked when he saw them. "You two are quite powerful when you do that, you know?"

"Spill," Alice ordered.

"I just needed some space."

"The ranch is all wide-open spaces." Alice waved her hand as if the idea were absurd.

"From Graham. And Calvin." He grimaced as he admitted that in front of Julia, but she sat with an understanding smile. "I understand he's the leader. He always has been. But sometimes he just doesn't listen. Seth and I have been trying to convince him to let us create a hunting program for the ranch. It'd be profitable, but it would need some start up costs and obviously a few improvements to the place before it could be established, but we've drafted the plans for it. Philip's helped us run the numbers and it could work. But Graham is adamant he doesn't want hunters on the place. That things are fine the way they are. Which I guess is true, but still, why not? It's another avenue of income and it would give Seth and me our own outlet. We're just hands at this point, but this would give us a place."

"A place of importance?" Alice asked.

"Somewhat, but also give us a chance to show what we can do."

"Well, you still have a few months before hunting season would even be starting. What do you do in the off season?"

"Plan, prep, but also still help around the ranch with other tasks. Just when hunting season comes about, our focus would be that."

"Interesting." Alice leaned back in the booth and glanced at Julia. Her friend shrugged as if the idea sounded fine to her. "And you've presented all of this to Graham?"

"Not the plans, just the idea."

"Ah. There's your problem." Alice snapped her fingers. "You realize Graham has to see a plan before he commits to anything, right?"

"He won't even give me a chance to present the plan. And then Cal shoots it down as well, which only reinforces Graham's dismissal."

"Let me worry about Calvin Hastings." Alice's eyes narrowed. "He and I are facing off on other issues at the moment, but I'm willing to throw myself at your service on this. I'll just add it to my list of grievances."

"Poor Cal," Julia whispered.

Alice smiled. "It's his own fault. Now, how long you going to keep this town job up?" she asked Clint.

"Today is my last day. I told Philip it wasn't for me. Which means tomorrow, I'll more than likely be helping build fence line." He didn't sound excited about the idea.

"Teamwork makes the dream work," Julia added.

Groaning, Alice and Clint chuckled as she blushed.

"What I mean is, work hard and help with the fence, and perhaps Graham and Calvin will be more open to what you have to say about the hunting idea."

"Doubt it, but thanks Julia." Feeling better, but still somewhat defeated in appearance, Clint polished off his drink and took a large chomp out of his sandwich.

Julia's phone dinged. "Speaking of my handsome cowboy." She smiled as she swiped her phone to read Graham's text message. "Dinner plans," she told them. "Hold on one second." She quickly typed her reply and then slipped her phone back into her purse. Her smile said it all when she returned back to the conversation.

"You love him, don't you?" Clint asked.

Baffled at his bold question, Julia flushed and blubbered to try and think of a response as Alice laughed. "She does."

"Yep. I can tell." Clint's slow smile had Julia relaxing.

"Just don't make a big deal about it, okay? I don't want Graham to feel pressured or anything in regards to our relationship." Suddenly shy, Julia took a sip of her tea.

"He's lucky," Clint said. "I don't get it. I mean, on your end at least. I love Graham and all, but I imagine it can't be or won't be easy to *love him*, love him. He's a tough shell."

"On the outside," Julia clarified. "On the inside, he's a big softie. Though don't tell him I said that or I will deny it. And don't act like he is, or he'll deny it. And I like that side of him." She perked up as Clint laughed.

"You're a good woman, Julia McComas." Winking at her, he took another bite of his sandwich. "Now we just need to find a good woman for Calvin."

"I'm working on that." Julia beamed and looked at Alice.

Clint choked on his bite as he registered her meaning. "You mean Al?" He coughed and patted his chest as he tried to recover from shock and laughter.

Alice frowned and crossed her arms again. "What's wrong with me?"

"You mean you're agreeable to this plan?" Clint asked.

"No, actually I am not, but I would still like to know why you think the idea is so ridiculous. I'm a great catch."

"Right. Yeah. I mean, sure. Of course you are. But Cal?" He shook his head. "I don't see it. You two drive each other crazy."

"True. I've told her it's a bad plan, but she doesn't get it." Alice munched on her chips as Julia rolled her eyes.

"My first thought was Ruby," Julia admitted, "but she's a little young and doesn't seem interested in Cal. Then I started observing Alice and his interactions, and I believe it could totally work, if this one would let her pride go."

"I like my pride."

"Pride's a sin, as Annie would say," Clint chimed in.

Alice rolled her eyes. "Yeah, well, the last person I want muddying up my life right now is Calvin Hastings. He already tries. Imagine if I gave him free rein. He'd be insufferable."

"I think he'd surprise you," Julia defended. "He's a sweetheart. All of you are," she told Clint. "Some of you just try to hide it and need a little help showing it."

"Cal? Sweet on Alice?"

"I didn't say he was... just that he could be, and I think it could work," Julia added.

"And I say no. And I'm sitting right here." Alice pointed at herself. "So let's move on. I'm eating and don't want to lose my appetite."

"*Your* appetite?" Clint tsked his tongue. "He's my brother. Discussing my brothers' potentials for romance is not my favorite topic either."

Julia shook her head as Alice and Clint laughed. "Fine. We'll eat in total silence and watch you make googly eyes at the waitress. That sounds like much more fun." Julia snickered as Clint's cheeks bloomed a bright pink and quietly shushed her as the waitress walked up to top off his drink.

H

Chapter Eight

"**When did you guys** lay out the pipes?" Calvin asked.

"Yesterday evening." Lawrence swiped a hand over his brow before placing his cowboy hat back on top of his head. He, along with Hayes, had tackled half a day's work the previous evening in order to avoid having to work it during the heat of the day. He liked that about Lawrence. He was always willing to put in the time if needed. And he did it mostly without complaining. And Hayes, well, he was up for most anything as long as it benefited the ranch. "Figured you and Graham would be working on the braces today. Hayes and I will start digging holes for the cedar posts."

"*You* will," Calvin corrected. "I don't want Hayes on the skid steer."

Lawrence laughed. "Got it."

"And Seth?" Calvin asked.

"Graham's got him up at Annie and Henry's today helping her with her yard work and landscaping."

"Good deal. Any news on Henry?" Calvin knew if there was news on anyone in town, much less their beloved Annie and Henry, Lawrence would know. His younger brother was one of the nosiest people he'd ever met. And the fact that he could charm a snake with a whistle meant Lawrence could fish information out of anyone if he wanted to. "Annie says he's recovering well, just that he's stubborn. Like she didn't already know that, but said it is a thousand times worse now that he's not able to be up and about as much."

"I do not envy her at the moment," Cal chuckled. "Or Seth having to handle their spats for the day."

Lawrence shook his head as Hayes rode up on his horse. He dismounted and tied the reins to the front grill guard of Lawrence's truck.

"That's your transportation for the day?" Cal asked.

"He needed to stretch his legs. And because he was eyeing the females a bit too much for my liking today, I needed to get him out of the pasture before he did something stupid."

Graham pulled up in his work truck and hopped out, his long legs eating up the walk in short time. He looked formidable, his jaw set, and his hat low. The oldest Hastings brother always had an air of authority about him, even when they were kids. When he looked up and saw Hayes's horse, he pointed to the water trough. "Better keep him hydrated."

"Already on it." Hayes pointed to a water bucket tied to his saddle.

"Cal and I will work braces, you two wi—"

"Already laid out the plans, Graham." Lawrence grinned. "You're late to the party. Probably because that pretty woman of yours had a late start heading to Sheffield this morning, no doubt."

Graham's face never changed expression as his brothers smirked at the teasing.

"Julia is not behind schedule. She was to pick up some supplies before heading into the clinic."

Lawrence shrugged. "I don't blame you for taking a few extra minutes." He winked as he started walking towards the truck and trailer that carried the cedar posts. "Come on, Hayes. I hear you get to drive the skid steer today." Lawrence turned on his heel to flash a mischievous grin at Calvin before hopping into the truck with his brother.

"What's with him today?" Graham asked.

"Just a good mood, I guess." Calvin rested his hands on his hips. "You good?"

"I'm fine." Graham looked annoyed at the question.

"Was just asking," Calvin chuckled. "You seem tense this morning."

"I'm fine," Graham assured him.

"Graham?" Calvin asked, tilting his head to survey his brother.

"Fine. I've just been thinking…"

"Thinking. I could see how that's strenuous." Laughing, Calvin slapped his brother's shoulder as they walked towards the first fence bracing.

"I want to marry her," Graham boldly stated.

"Is that what has you chewin' gravel this mornin'?"

Graham's eyes narrowed. He didn't see the humor in his situation as Calvin obviously did. "Oh come on, Graham, we all knew it would eventually head this direction. I'm happy for you. Have you talked to Julia about it?"

"No. Not since New Mexico."

"Well, what's stopping you?"

"I don't want to rush her. She hasn't been out here long."

"So? She loves you. You love her. I doubt she's planning on leaving. You might as well move right along with the happily ever after instead of just wastin' time."

"I'm not wasting time. I'm giving her time to adjust."

"More like giving yourself time to adjust." Cal grinned. He held up his hands to ward off Graham's glare. "Which is fine too. I think it's great you two found each other and I think it's smart to take your time. But don't wait too long, Graham. Because women like Julia don't come around too often."

Graham's answering harrumph had Calvin grinning. "And what about you?" Graham asked.

"What about me?"

"Haven't seen you on any dates lately."

"And when would I fit that in?"

"Wouldn't have to if you and Al decided to give it a go."

"What is with everyone trying to convince me that Alice and I should date?"

"Oh, so I'm not the only one who's noticed your special bond?" Graham smirked.

"Shut it. There is no special bond. In fact, she quite simply cut ties with me yesterday. Apparently I try to help her too much and she doesn't like it."

Graham lifted one of the pipes and waited patiently in silence as Calvin dropped his helmet and welded it into the steel pipe already fitted into the ground. He lifted his helmet and set the torch aside. "Nothing wrong with helping a friend," Graham continued.

"That's what I thought too, but apparently people were starting to talk and that bugged her."

"Alice has always been stubborn. She's never going to ask for help, and if she does it's through gritted teeth. I say help her any way. She'd have to be dumb and blind not to see she needs help with that little house."

"That's just it," Calvin handed Graham the beginnings of a roll of barbed wire. With Lawrence and Hayes having laid posts and now driving the posts in the ground, setting the first wire for the first stretch of fence line could easily be done. "I have a whole plan for her written out. I didn't even have a chance to show it to her before she jumped all over me for even going by her house."

Graham chuckled.

"What's so funny?"

"Cal, I say this lovingly, but don't be such a pushover."

"What?" Cal looked confused. "I thought I was being respectful by backing off."

"Alice is family. We don't back off. We help her. Even when she thinks she doesn't need it. That's what Annie would tell us."

"Right. Well, maybe I'm tired of having my hide chewed out over being willing to help."

"She hardly ever goes by the place. Just do the work and when you're done, show her."

"She won't like it."

"She'll get over it," Graham said. "Alice is one of us. We take care of our family and their property if need be. In the long run, it only benefits her having the house fixed up."

"I guess you're right," Calvin sighed. "I'll get started on it today after work."

"If you need help, ask Clint or Seth."

"You don't want me stealing Lawrence and Hayes?" Calvin laughed.

"No. I don't. Besides, Seth is pretty good with his hands and Clint just needs a project that distracts him from how much he abhors fence building. And hey, if there's a few of you working on it, Al can't get mad at just you. You're spreading the wrath."

"Now that, brother, is genius."

"I have my moments." Graham pointed to the next post. "Let's get moving. I don't want Lawrence and Hayes to grow arrogant that they're beating us."

Thankful for Graham's listening ear and advice, Calvin's mind already went into work mode on Alice's house. He knew what his first project would be, and that would be the AC situation. His plans would start today, and Graham was right, Alice would eventually accept the help. Family helped one another out.

∞

"Would you think me a terrible person if I did not show up for dinner tonight?" Alice asked.

Julia shook her head. "No, why?"

"Because I just want to pop some popcorn, have a soda, and watch television. I'm completely drained."

"Understandable." Julia grinned. "Remember when we'd do that every Sunday to watch that dystopian sci-fi show in college?"

"We never missed an episode."

"Still one of my favorite shows," Julia admitted. "You think Graham would like it?"

Alice laughed. "I think Graham would watch anything you wanted to watch."

"I might propose the idea tonight then. It would be fun to start a show together."

"Young love," Alice sighed wistfully as Julia nudged her shoulder on their way down the front steps of the clinic and to their separate vehicles. "See ya at the house."

"I'm stopping for a few groceries first, so it may be awhile for me. Graham said he'd be working late, so I'm taking advantage of his absence and doing a thorough grocery shopping trip."

"Don't forget the beer."

Julia chuckled. "As if I'd ever make that mistake. See ya later." She ducked into her red little sports car and backed out slowly onto the small side street off of Main.

Alice slid into her truck, her cell phone chiming. "This is Alice." She listened as a panicked patient relayed the woes of pet ownership and their dog that could not learn his lesson when it came to porcupines. She glanced at the clock. It was already close to six o clock, but she couldn't let a dog suffer overnight when she was still parked out front of the clinic. "Bring him in. I'm here." She hung up and thankfully did not have to wait long for the patient to arrive. The poor dog's face, covered in quills, had Alice shaking her head. "When are you going to learn, Boomer?" She lifted the overweight pit bull from his owner's arms and headed towards the back of the clinic. "Don't you know you will never win?" She gently stroked his side as she laid him on the table and gave him a sedative. Porcupine quills were not uncommon ailments. Dogs were curious, and when they stumbled upon the critters, they couldn't help themselves, and the results were always the same: quills to the face. Boomer was Alice's most popular patient for quills. He was five years old, and she'd successfully removed over 300 quills from his face over the last five years. She'd add another 43 to that today as she plucked away, checking his gums and nose to make sure she'd cleared the last of them. When she was sure she had, she lifted the unconscious dog and carried him out.

"Can't thank you enough, Doc."

"Did you at least shoot the pesky porcupine?" she asked.

"I did. They just seem to be everywhere."

"Well, his face is going to be sore."

"Yes ma'am." The man, Jay Thomas, loved Boomer. Alice knew Boomer would be rested in the house overnight and then catered to over the next few days, so her willingness to turn him over to Jay while he was still under the sedative was a no-brainer. Jay'd take care of him.

"Let him rest. He'll come to in an hour or so."

"Thanks, Doc."

"No problem, Jay. Take care." She watched as he drove away in his rusty old pickup truck and then turned back to the clinic to go clean up the exam room. When she finished, she decided a quick bite at Sloppy's on the way home was in order. She'd even call Ruby on her way so it would be hot and ready when she got there.

The call and the drive didn't take long. Her speed, she justified, was due to hunger and her eagerness to get home and indulge in her evening plans of popcorn gluttony. She pulled to a stop outside of Sloppy's and saw Calvin's truck behind the place. At her house. What was he doing there? Again. She thought she'd made herself clear. Annoyed, she climbed out of her truck and slammed the door.

"Ooooeeee young lady, I'd say you're in a fit." Roughneck Randy, gracing his usual spot on the front porch of Sloppy's, attempted a whistle through his sparsely toothed mouth. "I pity the man or woman in the path of your wrath tonight," he chuckled. "It's not me, is it?"

Alice shook her head, part of her fight leaving her as she smiled at Randy. Calvin could wait. She was hungry, and Randy, in his odd way, by pointing out her mood, made her realize that perhaps eating and calming down a minute was in her best interest. "Why don't you come inside, Randy? I'll buy you supper."

"Well, aren't you a quick turnaround." He grinned. "Ruby's already fed me. Twice. I'm as stuffed as a turkey on Thanksgiving mornin' and as satisfied as a sailor set for home. You head on in there and let her do the same for you."

Alice opened the door and Ruby waved her over to the bar. Hustling back into the kitchen, Ruby came back with the smothered steak and creamy mashed potatoes Alice had requested. The green beans, though not her favorite, were to make her feel better about herself for incorporating a vegetable.

"Long day?" Ruby asked.

"You could say that. Pretty tired."

"You look it."

"Thanks."

Ruby grinned. "Honesty is the best policy. I'm surprised you didn't wait for Calvin."

"Why would I wait for him?"

"Well, he called in his order not long after you. I assumed since he's out back at your place you two were going to eat together."

"You assumed wrong." Alice tried to keep the sting from her voice, but Ruby's brows rose and she waited for an explanation. "Sorry." Alice took a bite of her mashed potatoes. "Again... it's been a long day."

"No worries." Ruby smiled. "I get it. Oh, be right back." She hurried away as several men walked into the place and settled at a table in the corner.

Alice wasn't up for conversation, especially about Cal. And she was trying to muster enough energy and patience to deal with him after she finished the last of her steak. When she took her last sip of tea, she left money on the bar and walked out. Instead of driving around back, she walked towards her little house. *It did look a little sad*, she admitted. Even with lights on, the small place had an eerie and uninviting aura about it. She saw Cal inside, standing on a ladder. She opened the front door, the resounding creak oddly familiar and comforting. He looked down through his upstretched arms as he screwed in a light bulb.

"What are you doing?" Alice asked.

"Fixing this light." He finished turning the bulb and climbed down. He walked over to a cardboard box full of supplies he'd brought with him. She also noticed the attic door had been opened and the fold-out ladder descended to the ground floor. "What are you doing up there?"

"Mapping out your ventilation for central air and heat. I talked with Andy over in Sheffield, he can be here tomorrow to look it over and maybe get started on installation next week."

"I see." She also noticed she had a brand-new back door. A wooden screen door that had yet to be painted, the freshly sanded frame bright and cheerful against the dark painted walls. "You've been busy."

"Oh," He followed her gaze to the door. "yeah. Haven't painted it yet, though. Figured that could wait."

"What are you doing here, Calvin? I thought we discussed this?"

"We did. And then I had a conversation with Graham."

"Oh boy." Alice sighed and placed her hands on her hips. "And what did dear Graham have to say."

"He said to help you anyway. We're family. We help family. So here I am, helping."

"Even though I told you not to."

"Right."

"Do you not think that's just a smidgen pushy?"

"I guess so, but the way I figure it, it's also helpful." He flashed a quick smile before turning his attention back to his supply box.

Alice pinched the bridge of her nose. The Hastings brothers would be the death of her one day. She just knew it. "Cal—"

"I know. You're mad I didn't listen to you. You're mad I'm here. And you're mad that I'm *not* going to listen to you."

"That pretty much sums it up," Alice agreed. "I specifically told you not to do this. I don't know whether I'm mad at you or grateful to you, and both bug me. You didn't listen. I don't like not being listened to. And you didn't consult with me first."

"In my defense, I tried," he pointed out. "And you didn't listen to *me*."

"Not the point." She slashed her hand through the air as if his observation didn't matter.

"And if you're worried about what people will think, there's no harm there, because Seth and Clint agreed to help me. So it's not like people will get the wrong idea."

Great, she thought, *more brothers to deal with*. He looked pleased with himself, but not arrogantly so, just genuinely happy to help her. And she supposed he was. Cal liked helping people. He liked fixing things. He liked projects. Perhaps she was being too hard on him. He needed a side project and her house was an easy target. But she also hated taking advantage of the free labor.

"I'll pay you."

He looked horrified at the idea and that cracked her fierce resolve and a smile slipped through.

"Come on, Cal, you can't expect to do this all for free."

"I didn't even think on it."

"Of course you didn't." Alice patted his shoulder as if he were a simpleton. "You throw thousands of dollars into my house and you weren't expecting a penny in return?"

"I hadn't thought that far ahead. Besides, it doesn't matter to me. Just wanted to help you out."

She took a step towards him and he nervously flashed an apologetic smile. He held a screwdriver in one hand and light switch cover in the other. The cracked switch cover above her bar had bothered her for a while. Even something so little had not escaped his notice. "If you're going to work on my house, you have to discuss your plans with me."

"You mean you'll listen?"

She looked up at him and his eyes, a soft blue, reflected uncertainty and what seemed like nerves as she studied him. "I'll listen," she assured him. Her eyes, betraying her, flicked down to his lips before staring up at him again. What was it about this vulnerable side of Calvin that seemed so appealing?

He took a cautious step back and tossed the screwdriver into his box. "Then I think we should go over my plans." He reached for his clipboard and cleared his throat. He'd felt it too, she thought. The slight buzz between them, the shift in the air, the awkwardness. But he'd backed away. That should have been her first clue, but she felt like a magnet, attracted to him though they were polar opposites. She had to see. She had to see if there was something beneath their friendship. But how did she do that without jeopardizing years of friendship and family?

He slipped his pen from behind his ear and tapped it against the board. "So my first thought was that we'd convert the AC to central air and—" She silenced him with a quick press of her lips to his. She felt him tense. She pulled far enough away to look up at him. For a moment, his eyes searched hers. "What are you doing, Al?"

"Checking," she whispered.

"For what?"

"Anything different."

Calvin grunted and set his clipboard aside, his hands slightly fumbling with the pen as it rolled down the countertop. "I'll just leave this here and you can look over it."

Surprised at his lack of reaction, Alice tried to hide her embarrassment. "That's a good idea," she agreed. He avoided eye contact as he walked towards the door. *Great*, she thought. *She'd screwed things up.* She'd let Julia and Annie and Graham all get into her head and she'd messed up things with Cal, one of her best friends. But was she wrong? She couldn't be. She'd felt the hum between them, the tension, the subtle attraction that seemed to be brewing. She wasn't *that* out of practice when it came to men. She knew when attraction lurked beneath the surface. So why was Calvin walking away? Why did he not kiss her back? Plagued with doubt and upset at her own foolishness, Alice snatched the clipboard off the counter. Julia was about to get an earful.

H

Chapter Nine

Saturdays typically brought a half a day's work and then rest, but Graham felt the fence line was coming along well enough that everyone deserved the full weekend to rest and enjoy themselves. Calvin, Seth, and Clint were up at Alice's house. Clint worked on power washing the exterior and scraping away the loose paint. Seth was currently working on resettling the front porch and replacing the boards that suffered from rot. Cal was inside, knocking out all the smaller projects that seemed unnoticed, but added up. He was currently replacing the ceiling fan in the bedroom. The former fan, having lost two of its blades at some point, was not only an eyesore, but completely useless. Again, he was surprised Alice hadn't taken time to fix it or have it replaced. But she was hardly ever home. Perhaps that's why it wasn't much of a priority. She was extremely particular about her vet supplies. Her bags and gear were always organized, clean, and protected, but that attention did not carry over to her personal belongings. His hope, after they were done with the place, was that Alice would want to live in her home again or that she'd be proud enough to rent or sell it. Cal had an eye for design and construction, mostly because he enjoyed it. He'd drafted the plans for the guest house by Graham's, and with Annie's decorative help, they'd transformed it into a beautiful home. Julia had since placed a few of her personal touches upon the place as well. Alice, however, just slept there. He'd noticed her bag in the corner of the room and knew she hadn't left her own little house last night after he'd left. Surprised him, really, but she obviously felt safe enough to sleep in the place without new door locks in place.

He wondered if she needed space and time to think after she kissed him. She *kissed* him. *Him.* He still had trouble fathoming what had come over her. And he wasn't quite sure how she'd wanted him to react. It was nice. A little too nice. But he wasn't sure if that was because it was Alice or if it was the fact that he hadn't been kissed in quite some time. And though he considered acting upon his own urge to kiss her back, he didn't think it'd be fair to do so when he wasn't sure which feeling it was that he felt. So he left. He thought it was the honorable thing to do. He hadn't seen her since and therefore had no idea how their next interaction would go. She seemed to recover well enough, but he'd been so quick to jump ship he didn't really focus too much on her and what she might be feeling. Perhaps he could have handled it better. Sighing, he ran a hand over his hair. The sandy brown mixture was starting to curl above his collar, and he knew he needed a trim. He'd sweet talk Annie next time she was out at the ranch to give him a haircut.

"Fire in the hole!" Clint called out from outside.

The front door opened and shut with a bang as Ruby buzzed quickly into the small house carrying two large paper sacks. Rushing towards the kitchen counter, she laid her burden down. "Can't stay. In a hurry. Gotta get back. Lunch in the bags." She waved quickly and half walked, half jogged out the door as she hurried back to the restaurant.

"Did you call in lunch?" Calvin called to his brothers.

"Nope." Clint walked inside, scraping his boots on the threadbare rug by the door.

Seth's head emerged around the door jam. "Is that food?"

"Yep." Calvin waved him inside. "It would seem Ruby is taking care of us today."

"I like when Sloppy takes care of us." Clint held up a boxed slice of pie. "She does it so well."

Seth grinned. "Cherry. That's my favorite."

"We'll have to remember to drop some money off later," Calvin suggested.

"I'll take care of it," Clint said. "Lawrence and I had planned to eat supper at Sloppy's later."

"Good deal."

"What's with the women in our lives?" Seth asked. "Julia likes cooking for us. Alice is our own personal doctor when need be. Annie checks on us like a mother, and Sloppy tends to us when she can. Are we lucky? Blessed? Or cursed to have such overly attentive females in our lives?"

"Are you complaining about female attention?" Clint's brows shot into his hairline. "Are you alright up there?" He tapped a finger against Seth's temple.

Seth ducked away from his brother's touch and swatted Clint's hand. "Not complaining, just pointing out an observation."

"I don't mind the extra attention," Clint grinned. "Until I find my own woman, it's kinda nice having at least some female lovin'. And my stomach doesn't complain from all the nice meals. I had lunch with Julia and Alice in Sheffield yesterday. Man, there was this pretty little waitress—"

"Wait, what?" Calvin asked. "You went to lunch with them?"

"Yeah. I was there, saw them, joined them. It was surprisingly kind of fun." Clint studied Cal's face. "Jealous?"

"What? No." He shook his head, but a small slip of awkwardness betrayed his hands as he began unpacking the lunch sacks and dropping several items a couple of inches above the countertop.

Seth and Clint exchanged curious glances.

"So, Al wasn't at the guest house this morning," Seth added. "Jewels said she stayed here last night. Weren't you workin' over here?" he asked Calvin.

"For a bit." Still no eye contact.

"I see." Seth crossed his arms and nodded towards Clint to take over the interrogation of their brother's odd behavior.

Obliging, Clint took his meal to the small dining table and set up shop. He took a large bite of his grilled chicken sandwich before plunging into full interrogation mode. "Was Al surprised to see you here?"

"A bit." Calvin took a sip of the syrupy sweet tea Ruby'd brought over. It never ceased to satisfy.

"And?"

"And what? She was aggravated again, at first, and then decided that our help wasn't such a bad idea."

"That it?"

"Why wouldn't it be?" Cal challenged, but his flushed face told his brothers there was more to the story.

"She kissed you, didn't she?" Seth asked, his face slowly splitting into a wide grin.

Baffled, embarrassed, and a bit annoyed, Calvin ignored the question.

"She totally did, didn't she?" Clint guffawed and slapped his knee. "Julia is going to have a field day when she hears this."

"It was nothing. A silly slip-up."

"Did you kiss her back?" Seth asked. "Was it nice? Weird? Is Alice a good kisser?" His questions shot like buck shot, one after another covering a wide array of spread as they showered over Cal.

"Stop it. It was nothing. Nothing happened afterwards either."

"You didn't kiss her back?"

"No."

"Why not?" Clint asked. "I bet that ruffled her feathers."

"Because it wasn't right," Cal said. "Now let's drop this."

"No way." Seth beamed. "Alice... kissing." He pulled a face. "Just never quite pictured her the lovey dovey type."

"She is not lovey dovey," Calvin interrupted and then growled as his brothers' cheesy grins encouraged him to tell them more. He shook his head. "Just drop it. It happened. Nothing is going to come from it. We all move on."

"Right." Clint grabbed his cell phone. "Right after I tell Julia." He typed a quick text and as Calvin lunged towards the phone, Clint tossed it to Seth. Seth quickly darted from his chair out of Cal's reach to finish the text and hit send.

Little brothers, Cal thought, *were champions at annoying the older ones.*

∞

"Well, I did it. I kissed him!" Alice yelled as she stormed inside the guest house and waited for the boisterous squeal from Julia. Instead, silent and surprised faces stared back at her. Julia, Annie, and Graham sat in the living room.

"Well, well, well." Annie reached for her glass of sweet tea and sipped from her straw. "I don't know who *him* is, but do tell." She winked as she waited for Alice to continue.

Julia laughed as Graham fidgeted in his chair at the turn in conversation.

"Beat it," Alice told him, and he obediently obliged, giving Julia a quick peck on the cheek as he donned his hat and hurried his steps towards the door to avoid her sudden urge for girl talk.

Julia affectionately watched him leave.

"Now who stole your lips, honey?" Annie asked. "Don't leave a gal in suspense."

Growling in frustration, Alice plopped down in Graham's empty seat. "Calvin."

Annie, not prepared for her reply, choked on her tea. She coughed into her hand a couple of times to regain her composure. "Well... that is somethin'."

The squeal Alice knew would happen erupted from Julia's lips. "And?"

"And what?"

"How was it?" Julia asked.

"It was a simple peck on the lips."

"How'd he react?"

"He left."

Julia's face fell. "He left?"

"Yep. He didn't say much afterwards, but he sure high-tailed it out of there."

Annie hooted in laughter. "Poor sweet Calvin."

"Poor Calvin?" Alice looked offended. "I was the one standing there looking like an idiot."

"Oh honey," Annie patted Alice's knee. "you probably just surprised him. I mean, why did you even consider kissin' him?"

"You ask me that after our conversation at the hospital? Julia's planted it in my head that there's more to Calvin and me than just friendship."

"Planted?" Julia rolled her eyes. "I said there's chemistry."

"And there is... was," she corrected. "Until I screwed it up by plantin' one on him."

"Calvin's a thinker," Annie reminded her. "You probably just took him by surprise is all. He'll need time to mull it over."

"All I know is that I can't handle awkwardness. And it was definitely awkward afterwards. And I told him he could work on my house. I'm sure he's there now with Clint and Seth. And as much as I want to check on things, I don't think I can look him in the eye right now."

Julia's phone dinged and she picked it up. A laugh escaped her lips as she showed it to Annie.

"Like I said," Annie proudly sat up straighter. "He's a thinker. He's already discussing it with his brothers."

Alice's face blanched. "What?" She snatched the phone and her cheeks deepened in color. "Great. Now everyone is going to know."

"Don't freak out." Julia sent a quick reply to Clint and then focused back on her friend. "It's a good sign. It means he did not completely dismiss you."

"Well it sure felt that way. I don't like rejection."

"Who does?" Annie asked. "But trust me, honey, that boy is too sweet a person to let a little ol' kiss come between years of friendship."

"I just shouldn't have done it." Alice leaned back in the chair, sprawled, legs outstretched, and chin slouched against her chest.

"Well it's no reason not to act like a lady," Annie scolded, nodding towards Alice's sitting position. Alice acquiesced and sat up, though she leaned her chin in her hand.

"Anyways, let's talk about something else. I can't think about it anymore. It just makes me feel crummy."

"I'm sorry it wasn't all bells and whistles." Julia looked disappointed.

"I didn't say it was bad," Alice told her and had her friend's eyes sparking in curiosity. "Just that he didn't respond."

"So it was good?" Julia asked.

"Well, for as simple of a kiss as it was, yeah, it wasn't bad. He has surprisingly soft lips."

Julia and Annie laughed and Alice finally smirked.

"Already an upside." Annie nodded in approval.

"I've just never had a man walk away from me like that before. That stung."

"Consider it flattering. He had to take a moment to collect himself because he liked it too and is trying to figure it out."

"About as flattering as self-cut bangs, feels like."

Julia bit back a chuckle. "Yes, well... we shall see how things unfold, I guess. Tomorrow."

"What's tomorrow?"

Annie eyed Alice in disapproval. "Church, young lady, and then lunch at my house. Or have you forgotten?"

"Oh, right. I don't know if—"

"Don't you dare refuse," Annie interrupted. "Henry needs his kiddos around. Keeping up with our normal Sunday meal will do wonders for his spirits. And mine. That man is driving me crazy right now. He needs to see you all to have someone new to talk to. I can only handle so many discussions about Jeopardy. And boy, does he watch it every day now that he's reduced to his recliner for rest right now."

"And what did he do before?"

Annie paused. "Well, he watched Jeopardy, but he didn't quiz me every five minutes. He'd watch it and then go dally in the garden."

Alice grinned. "I like it when Henry drives you crazy."

"And why is that?" Annie asked, sass lining her words.

"Because you secretly love it."

"Yes, well, secretly love it meaning I'm going to beat him over the head with my copy of Better Homes and Gardens if I hear, "What is the Egyptian God Nubius," one more time."

"Is that his answer for everything?" Julia asked on a laugh.

"Oh, Lord no, just that he always answers the questions out loud. And annoyingly so, because he's usually right."

"Young love," Alice chuckled as they heard truck doors closing and could see Clint and Seth walking towards Graham's porch.

"Looks like the boys are back." Julia leaned towards the blinds and peaked through to see Calvin's truck pulling up as well. "And look who it is." She wriggled her eyebrows at Alice.

Groaning, Alice waved Julia's hand away from the blinds. "Don't let him see you."

"Oh, Calvin!" Annie, quicker than a pistol shot was already at the door and waving him over.

"What the—" Alice darted to her feet and looked for room to escape as Julia laughed and pointed towards her own bedroom so that Alice would not have to cross behind Annie to reach her own.

Boots clomping on steps spoke of Cal's arrival. "This is a nice surprise." Cal hugged Annie, removing his hat a moment as he did so, the polite gesture engrained in his blood. He nodded a greeting towards Julia before placing his hat back on his head.

"I was bored," Annie told him. "And I needed time with my girls."

"Beautiful company, who could blame you?"

"Now, I was checking the house and noticed a couple things. Would you mind?" Annie motioned him inside and shut the door.

Julia sat, a smug smile on her face as she watched Annie in action. No surprise, Annie walked him towards Julia's bedroom. "The knobs on the tub seem to be leaking in Julia's bath."

"Hmmm." Cal turned to walk back towards his truck. "Let me grab my screwdriver. They may just need to be tightened up again."

"Oh no." Annie forcefully turned his shoulders back towards the bedroom. "You should look at it first."

"But—" He continued keeping pace so as not to trip as she shoved him through the bedroom door and closed it behind him. She swiped her hands together. "That ought to get them talkin'."

Julia softly clapped her hands. "I am continually impressed by you, Annie."

Winking, Annie walked back over to her seat and toasted her tea glass to Julia's. "Years of experience, sweetie."

H

Chapter Ten

Cal stumbled into Julia's bedroom, looking back at the closed door as if he'd stepped through a portal. *What in the world was up with Annie?* he thought.

His eyes adjusted to the room as he caught a flash of movement by the window. Alice turned and surprise had her mouth agape. "What are you doing in here?"

"Annie said Julia's tub needed work."

Alice crossed her arms in disapproval. "And you fell for it?"

"She seemed legitimately concerned. I'm guessing it's not true." Calvin rubbed a hand over his jaw. "You told her, didn't you?"

"On accident," Alice admitted.

Cal looked at the ceiling in frustration.

"Don't be mad at me. You told Clint and Seth."

"I didn't. They guessed."

"What are we, in the sixth grade?" Alice stomped her way towards the bedroom door, Calvin gently grabbing her elbow before she passed by him.

"I'm not mad, you know." He looked down into her bright blue eyes. He could see her temper slowly ebbing away. "Just surprised was all."

"Right. Well, it happened. It's over. Nothing to talk about." She started to reach for the knob again and he tugged her back towards him.

"Why'd you do it?" he asked. "And no lies." He watched as uncertainty played across her face.

"I was curious. With several people mentioning it seemed like we would be… well, that we could be a good match, I thought I would see. I mean, you're one of my best friends, isn't that who you're supposed to look for when looking for a special someone? A friend? Someone you enjoy spending time with?"

"And are you looking for someone special?"

"Not exactly. I mean, I wasn't. I just… I just thought there'd been some chemistry," she mumbled, looking down at her feet. "Clearly, I was wrong, and that's fine. I'm fine with just being friends. I don't want you to think I need or want more than that."

"So, you don't want more than friendship?" He was trying to understand but having a difficult time. Patience, he reminded himself.

She exhaled and her bangs fluffed off of her forehead. The stereotypical Alice gesture made him smile. "Just forget about it all, Cal."

"So it was absolutely nothing? Meant absolutely nothing?"

"Yeah, I guess so." Alice looked up at him. "Are we cool?"

He felt like there was more to say. Her easy dismissal of the situation kind of irked him, but what was he to say? If she said she didn't have feelings for him, he should just believe her, right? Move on as she wants. But something didn't ring true in her words. But he still wasn't sure how he felt about Alice even possibly having feelings for him, so he wasn't sure he wanted to open the door to that conversation yet either. So he let it go. "Yeah. We're cool." He pulled her into a tight hug and gave her a squeeze. He would remember later as he took a shower just how her hair smelled and, though he wanted to ignore it, how well she'd fit in his arms.

∞

Henry took a long and satisfied gulp of his sweet tea before setting his glass on the small table next to his recliner. "How's the fence comin'?"

Hayes leaned back against the couch cushions and sighed in contentment, his stomach full and his sweet tooth satisfied thanks to Annie, Julia, and Alice. He looked to Graham, but his older brother was distracted by Julia. "Good," he answered on behalf of the others.

"You still training that awful horse?" Henry asked him.

"When I can. Mostly in the evenings."

"Cal, you got that loader up and running yet?"

"No. I'm waiting on some parts. Not a big deal though, we haven't had too big a need for it lately."

"Alice?" Henry turned slightly in his chair and looked over his shoulder.

"What you need, Henry?" She walked over and he gently clasped her hand.

"Be a dear and top off my glass, will you?"

"Of course." She pointed to the brothers. "Anyone else?"

Lawrence held up his cup and she nodded before darting away to grab the tea pitcher. She went ahead and topped off all their glasses and Annie walked in with a tray of cookies and placed them on the center coffee table in the den. "Help yourselves, kids. I've been on a baking spree and Henry needs help clearing out my cookie jar."

"You've already stuffed us full of pudding, Annie." Cal rubbed his stomach but accepted the napkin the fiery older woman handed him.

"Alice, pass the tray, and make sure Calvin eats double."

He groaned as he accepted two large chocolate chip cookies and began to nibble on the first one. Alice nodded in approval as she handed Hayes two peanut butter cookies, his favorite. Julia grabbed cookies for her and Graham. Alice swatted her friend's hand when she reached for the last chocolate chip one. Julia chuckled and immediately diverted her attention to a lemon square.

Alice set the tray down and plopped onto the couch, landing between Clint and Calvin. Clint wriggled his eyebrows at her and nodded towards his brother. She rolled her eyes. It'd take a while before things fully felt normal again since everyone seemed to know she'd busted a move on Cal. So far though, Calvin himself acted fine. He was his normal self, though possibly a bit quieter, but she also knew he was exhausted. So that could be the main factor. She hoped.

"When does the new guy start at the clinic, Alice?" Henry asked. "'Bout time you got some help."

"He's coming Monday to work a few days to see if it is a good fit."

"What new guy?" Cal asked.

"Oh, a vet tech that contacted Philip. Julia's flyers seem to actually work." Alice toasted towards her friend. "Our first bite of someone willing to work in Sheffield."

"Who is it?" Cal continued his interrogation.

Alice shrugged. "Some guy named Jimmy. He's from east Texas somewhere."

"Why's he moving out here?"

"I don't know. I didn't ask."

"Well, seems a little random."

"Don't steal her thunder, Cal," Philip warned. "Al needs help and this guy seemed genuinely excited about the opportunity."

"Have any of you checked him out?" Cal looked to his brothers, his protective streak towards Alice showing loud and clear.

Julia bit back a smile as she whispered something to Graham.

The brothers shook their heads. Philip raised his hand. "I at least checked out his credentials before I referred him to Alice. I didn't want to waste her time on some fresh out of school kid, but this guy seems to be knowledgeable and has steadily worked at the same veterinarian office in east Texas for the last five years. He seems to know what he's doing."

"Dad will be there too," Alice added. "To gauge his feelings on the guy, so that's helpful."

"Is he single?" Calvin asked.

"I don't know." Alice, confused as to why it would matter, cast him a dumbfounded look. "Why?"

"Just curious. I mean, you and Julia work mostly alone up there. It'd be nice to know his character a bit before you girls are stuck in an awkward situation."

"How about this?" Alice turned to face him. "You can show up bright and early Monday morning and quiz him on his intentions. I'm sure he'd appreciate that and I'm also sure it wouldn't send him runnin' at the first opportunity. It may have escaped your notice, Cal, but Julia and I are grown women. We can take care of ourselves."

"And Doc Wilkenson will be there, like she said," Seth reminded him.

"Exactly. I doubt the new guy is going to bust a move when my dad is there." Alice smirked towards Julia. "I'm excited. I'm ready for some help."

Cal seemed to be the only brother irked by the new turn of events, which was interesting. He'd made it clear he didn't see her as more than a friend, yet he was worried about some stranger sweeping her off her feet. It didn't make sense. Then again, he'd always been protective of her. When she was eight and Steven Rogers, an eye catching ten-year-old, had decided he wanted to marry her, Calvin put a stop to that rather quickly. He'd personally backed Steven up against the swing set on the playground and said if any ten-year-old was going to marry Alice it'd be him, *not* a Rogers. She grinned at the memory. Calvin had always been there for her in some form or fashion, so she'd let his outburst slide. This time.

"Next Friday, don't forget," Annie interrupted. "we girls are going to Fort Stockton to shop. So, no birthing calves, neutering horses, or tumorous pigs better stand in the way of our girls' day, Alice Wilkenson."

Alice held up her hand in scout's honor. "I shall do my best."

"Tumorous pigs?" Julia looked disgusted. "That's about as gross as the tumorous rats."

Graham chuckled as he squeezed her hand in his. "It takes a special stomach to handle those."

"Seriously. I've seen some of the oddest things since working at the clinic. Some gross, and some just plain weird. And it doesn't help that whenever something disgusting or horrifying comes in, Alice calls me back into the exam room."

"You should know by now," Alice laughed.

"I do know. And I brace myself in the hallway before I walk inside. It's good for me to know what procedures or problems you handle. I just... don't always like to see them so up close." Julia shimmied her shoulders and grimaced.

"You've gotten better. It's hard to shock you now." Alice grinned. "But I'm still going to try."

"Well, divert that attention to the new guy for a bit and give my heart and stomach a break."

"You don't want to run Julia off, Alice," Annie warned. "She's been a Godsend to you and to Graham. And if you run her off, Graham and all of us will have your hide."

"It'll take more than Alice's pranks and teasing to run me off." Julia leaned her head affectionately on Graham's shoulder. "I don't plan on going anywhere."

"We won't let you," Hayes replied.

"Yep. You're stuck with us," Lawrence added. "And Graham."

Julia beamed as Annie gently rested her hand on Henry's shoulder and stood behind his chair. Alice loved this group of people. If her dad were with them, it'd be a complete picture of her family. Not all of the same blood, but family. And Julia did complete it. She was perfect for Graham. Now, the other brothers just needed to find good women and she could possibly find a decent man to settle down with and their wonderful hodge-podge family could grow. When Calvin asked her about finding someone special, she hadn't much considered it. It wasn't on her agenda, but the more she thought about it, the more she was open to it. Clearly, it wasn't Calvin, but she wasn't closed off to potentially putting herself out there. Only time would tell. In the meantime, she had a possible new work partner that would need to be trained, and if she wanted it to work out, she needed to focus all of her brain power on training him how she wanted.

∞

"Just drive it in by hand." Graham, along with all the other brothers besides Seth and Hayes, were driving the cedar posts into the correct positions along the fence line. Seth opted for driving the skid steer to drill holes with the auger ahead of the line. Hayes walked alongside him to make sure he dug in the right spots. Clint and

Lawrence tackled posts further down the line. Even with the head start by Lawrence and Hayes the previous week, there was still over a mile of fence line to complete.

It was strenuous and sweltering work driving posts in the heat of summer, two brothers to a post. Graham slammed the post driver down on top of the cedar post as Calvin held it lightly in his hands to secure it in place. With the heat bearing down on them, Cal felt like he wiped sweat out of his eyes every five seconds. Graham brushed his temple with his elbow before slamming the driver down once more. Cal bent down and poured the rock and dirt into the hole to pack it in and hold the post up. He stood, and both brothers took a deep breath before heading to the next post and switching positions.

"So how do you feel about this new guy at the clinic?" Cal glanced at his brother as Graham rested his hands on the post and waited for Calvin to drive it into the dirt.

"I think it will be good. Alice needs the help. Julia seems excited about the idea. Why?"

"Just wonderin'." Cal slammed the driver down.

Graham watched as Calvin raised his arms and drove down the steel driver with more force than necessary. "I take it you're not that thrilled about it." A smile briefly flashed across Graham's face.

"I didn't say that."

"You don't have to. Your objections yesterday and your question just now says otherwise. You still thinkin' about that kiss?"

"What kiss?"

"The one Alice planted on ya." Graham held up his hand to ward off Cal's denial. "One, I was there when Alice confessed to it. And two, Julia is still holding onto hope that it meant something to both of you. So don't act like it didn't happen."

Cal heaved a tired sigh as he and Graham moved to the next post. "I've been thinkin' on it, yeah. I mean, how could I not? Sort of changes things a bit."

"Does it?"

"Well, yeah. I didn't realize Alice would even consider something more than friendship, especially with me. And I'd be lying if I didn't admit to there being some chemistry there. There always has been. I just chalked it up to us being good buddies."

"And that could be it," Graham suggested. "But gives a good foundation, should you choose to make it one."

"Yeah, that's what I've been thinkin' on. I mean, I care about her, you know? Always have. Ever since her momma left and Doc Wilkenson had his hands full at the clinic, I made sure to look out for her. It's sort of nailed into who I am now. I will always look out for her."

"But that doesn't mean you care for her as more than a friend."

"But the thing is," Cal continued. "I *want* to look out for her. I like doing it." He scratched the stubble on his chin before slamming the post driver down again. "And I sure don't want some vet tech thinkin' he can just slide into the picture."

Graham hid his smile as he crouched to fill the hole around the bottom of the post. "I doubt he busts a move on Alice. She wouldn't stand for it."

"What if they hit it off?"

Graham stood to his feet and dusted his hands on his pant legs. "Look, Cal, if you think you have feelings for Alice then you need to either act on them or move on. Alice made the first move, so the ball is in your court now. If the kiss meant nothing to you or you didn't feel any level of attraction towards her after it, then it's best to move forward as friends. But, if you did feel more or it unsettled you enough to consider more than friendship, then you need to man up and ask Alice out."

"Out where?"

"Anywhere." Graham removed his work gloves a moment as he began picking a thorn out of one of the finger sleeves.

"But if things don't work out, we'd lose her."

"Is that what you're worried about?" Graham looked up. "You're nervous things will fall apart and we'll lose our closest friend?"

"It's exactly what I'm worried about. That and that I'm being completely foolish to even consider all of this."

"I can't help you there. All I can do is give you a bit of advice."

"I'm listening..." Calvin rested his hands on his hips as he brushed his sleeve over his forehead.

"With Julia, I didn't want to admit I had feelings for her, to myself or anyone else. But when I realized I did have feelings for her, I couldn't let her slip through my fingers. So as uncomfortable as it made me feel at the time, it was the best move I ever made. But it was a calculated move. I knew that I could potentially screw up my friendship with Alice by dating her friend. What if it didn't work out? What if Julia didn't feel the same way and up and slapped me when I kissed her? In the end, the risk outweighed the worry, because she was too special to pass up. So ask yourself, is Alice too special to pass up? If she ended up with someone else, would you kick yourself for not giving it a shot?" Graham walked towards the next post and Calvin instinctively followed. "That's all I have to offer you."

Calvin appreciated Graham's honesty. Graham wasn't one to share his feelings or thoughts much. Cal appreciated his brother's openness. "I just never even considered Alice, you know? I mean, she's been right in front of me this whole time. Could it have really been that simple? And if so, look at all the time we've wasted."

"It's not wasted time if you two didn't realize there was more there in the first place. Stop beating yourself up. The question you have to ask yourself now is, what do you want to do now?"

"Call me crazy, but I haven't stopped thinking about that kiss. As innocent as it was, it's been haunting me."

"Then I think you have your answer." Graham pointed to the post in front of him. "Can we get back to work now?"

Laughing, Cal nodded, not in the least embarrassed for calling upon his older brother's listening ear.

H

Chapter Eleven

"He's great, isn't he?" Alice whispered to Julia as Jimmy followed her dad into an exam room to see another patient. "I mean, he's knowledgeable, friendly, and willing to jump in where needed."

"I think he seems competent," Julia agreed. "And I like his personality, so I could see him fitting in around here."

"Yeah, me too." Alice beamed. "Yay!" She danced a small jig in place as she grabbed the next folder from Julia. "Will be nice to have some help." She looked up and turned towards the waiting area. "Sparkles."

A college-aged girl stood up with a teacup chihuahua, the little dog boasting a jewel-encrusted collar and painted nails. Alice dreaded chihuahuas, much less the tiny ones. They were delicate animals. Small dogs in general were, but teacup varieties faced challenges larger breeds did not, mostly with their digestive tracts. The girl followed her to an exam room and she shut the door. As predicted, the dog had swallowed a marble. Thankfully, the girl brought her in immediately and with a little induced vomiting, Sparkles was able to pop the marble out of her mouth and not have to have a surgery to remove it from her intestines or stomach. Alice walked back towards the waiting room and startled at the sight of Calvin leaning on the reception desk chatting with Julia.

"What are you doing here?" Alice asked, her hand quickly smoothing over her hair of its own volition.

Calvin straightened as Julia giggled. "He brought puppies!" She held one up as it licked her chin. "Aren't they adorable?"

"Puppies?" Alice looked at the box by his feet and spotted several mixed breed puppies climbing on top of one another for attention. "Where did you find those?"

"Someone dumped them on the highway. I was headed into town to pick up parts for the loader and saw them on the side of the road."

"Well you have the wrong place," Alice told him. "The shelter is two blocks over."

"I'm not taking them to the shelter."

"Oh really?" Alice looked into the box again. "And what are you going to do with, 1-2-3-4-5-6-7-8 puppies?"

"One for each of us," he grinned.

"There are only seven Hastings brothers last I counted."

"Sloppy already said she wanted one as well."

"You've already seen Ruby today?"

"Grabbed a coffee for the road. She was all about them. I told her she could have first pick." Calvin ruffled the fur of the puppy in Julia's hands.

"I see." Alice crossed her arms. "And why did you bring them here?"

"I figured they needed first round of shots and deworming."

Calvin looked up as Jimmy and Doc Wilkenson walked into the room. Doc's face lit up. "Calvin Hastings, good to see you, son." Her dad heartily shook Cal's hand. "What brings you by?"

Cal pointed to the puppy in Julia's hands and to the box at his feet.

"Now, I say, that's a load." Doc Wilkenson bent down and scooped up one of the puppies. "Looks like a decent mix, maybe Australian Shepherd with a little lab or retriever thrown in. Where'd you find these little guys?"

"On the highway headed into town."

"I'd say there's just enough for you boys to each have one."

"That's my thought as well. We haven't had a dog on the ranch in years."

"And now you want seven?" Alice shook her head. "Graham would never go for it."

Cal nodded towards Julia snuggling the pup in her arms. "Wanna bet?"

Alice smiled. "You have a point."

"Al, why don't you and Jimmy get these little guys vaccinated. I'll handle the waiting room."

Alice pointed to the box of puppies and Cal lifted it into his arms. Julia gently placed the puppy back inside as Jimmy rounded the corner. "We have puppies," Alice ordered, pointing down the hall to an exam room.

"First round?" Jimmy asked.

"Yep."

"I'll get them."

"Eight all together."

Jimmy saluted and walked in the opposite direction.

"So that's the new guy, hm?" Cal asked.

"Yep. I like him."

"So you think you'll keep him?"

"If he wants to stay, yes. He's good."

"Seems pretty young."

"Just a couple years younger than me," Alice stated. "Not that young."

Jimmy walked into the room carrying a tray of syringes and medicine vials. "These are cute little guys." He stuck his hand in the box and the puppies tackled one another for attention. Jimmy extended his other hand towards Cal. "Jimmy Williams."

"Calvin Hastings."

"Ah. Hastings... you Julia's boyfriend?"

Cal shook his head. "I do not have that privilege. That would be my older brother, Graham."

"Ah. She said there were a lot of you."

"You'll meet them all tonight, I'm sure," Alice said.

"Tonight?" Calvin asked.

"Julia's invited us over for dinner at Graham's."

"Us? As in everyone?"

"You didn't get the message?"

"Apparently not." Calvin checked his phone.

"Maybe you're not invited," Alice teased and stuck out her tongue.

Smirking, Cal tilted his head. "That wouldn't be quite fair would it?"

"You'd probably just show up anyway, uninvited. You're good at that."

Jimmy's eyes bounced between the two of them as they drilled into one another.

"Ouch." Calvin feigned a wounded expression. "And here I was in Sheffield, picking up more supplies for your house, trying to be a good friend."

She rolled her eyes and then looked to Jimmy. "Alright, let's do this."

Jimmy picked up a puppy and Alice did the same. Between the two of them, the puppies were all taken care of in just a few minutes. "Which one do you plan on keeping?" Alice asked.

Shrugging, Calvin looked them all over. "Whichever is left, I guess, after everyone else picks."

It was so like Cal to let everyone else have their choice before him.

"All done." Alice placed the last puppy in the box. "And what are you going to do if a momma dog shows up looking for her puppies?"

"Take her in. Obviously the person who dumped them doesn't want them." Cal lifted the box with ease and walked towards the main lobby. "Thanks for taking care of them."

"You bet."

"It was nice to meet you," Jimmy called, before heading into an exam room with Doc Wilkenson. Cal nodded in farewell to the man as he flashed a smile at Julia. "How much do I owe this one?" He tilted his head towards Alice.

"Nothing," Alice said.

"What?" Cal and Julia both looked surprised.

"You heard me."

"I did, but why?"

"Look, don't make a big deal about it," Alice warned. "You're working on my house for free, it's the least I can do."

"Well, thanks, Al." Cal pulled her to his side with one arm and gave her a friendly squeeze.

"Oh, and Cal," Julia interrupted. "I'm cooking tonight, so be sure to come for dinner."

Cal looked down at Alice.

"Don't look so smug." Alice's shoulders squeezed together as he gave her another tight hug and he laughed.

"I'll see you ladies then. I've got some more errands to run and then deliveries to make." He held up the box of puppies. "Have a good rest of the day."

He walked out of the building and down the front steps, Alice leaning to the right to watch his departure.

"Ahem." Julia cleared her throat and sat with her arms crossed and a satisfied smile. "Is there something you needed, Doctor Wilkenson?"

She could hear Julia's soft laugh behind her as Alice murmured an impolite comment on her way towards the break room.

∞

"I don't need a dog. In fact, the last thing I need is a dog," Graham barked as he carried two fresh cases of beer into his house and stocked his refrigerator.

"Julia's going to be mighty disappointed," Calvin reported. "Seems this one stole her heart today at the office." Cal picked up a small brown puppy, its fear of being held above the floor causing it to whine in his hand.

"You already showed Julia?" Graham asked.

"She does work there."

"That was a sneaky move." Graham rubbed his chin. "Fine. I'll see how he… is it a he or a she?"

Cal tipped the puppy over. "He."

"Fine. We'll see how he and Curly get along, but if he's mean to my cat, he goes."

Cal grinned. "Congrats. You're the proud new owner of…. what are you going to name him?"

"I don't know. Figure Julia can since she's so enamored with him as you say she is."

Nodding, Calvin flagged down Hayes as his brother was headed towards home. Hayes pulled his truck to a stop in front of Graham's. "I was hoping to shower before dinner."

"You still have time." Cal walked over to his brother's window. Reaching into the box he pulled out a puppy and handed it to him. "Merry Christmas, Happy Birthday, Happy Valentine's."

"What is this?" Hayes fumbled the puppy a moment before stroking a hand over its head.

"A gift. Everyone gets one." Calvin pointed to Graham's newest pup already asleep in his arms.

"Nice. Thanks." Hayes peeked underneath the puppy's tail. "A girl. I'll have to think of a pretty name. Where'd you find these?"

"On the side of the road."

Hayes's puppy licked his chin. "Oh now, that's terrible." His voice took on a lulling quality as if he were talking to an infant. "No one treats my girl like that."

Laughing, Calvin tapped a hand on the windowsill to send his brother off towards home. He tossed his thumb over his shoulder. "See? Not so hard to convince the others to take one."

"That was Hayes. He is an easy target when it comes to taking animals in. Good luck with Philip."

"Already dropped one off to Philip on the way home."

Graham's face blanched a moment. "He took one?"

"Yep. Said it'd be great to have one around the store."

"Wow. You're better at this than I gave you credit for."

Tapping the edge of his hat to signal his departure, Calvin slid the box into his front passenger seat. "Gotta go make more deliveries."

"Good luck."

Cal watched as Graham brushed his cheek over the puppy's head as he carried him into the house. His next target was Lawrence. And as luck would have it, his brother was just stepping out of his truck in front of his house when he pulled up, Seth with him. He pulled to a stop and had them both turning.

"What's up?" Lawrence walked towards Cal's driver side window, his eyes widening as he spotted the puppies.

"Want one?"

"Do you even have to ask?" Lawrence grinned as he walked towards the passenger door and opened it to better view his options. "Any of them spoken for?"

"Nope. Ruby claimed hers, Graham his, Philip snatched one, and Hayes just took his home. Feel free to take your pick."

"I like this spotted one." Lawrence picked up the squirming puppy and a stream of urine poured onto his shirt. "Well, now that wasn't nice," he laughed as he rested it in the crook of his arm.

"Got them their first round of shots today."

"Good deal."

"Want one?" Cal looked to Seth.

"No thanks."

"Really?"

"Yep. One dog in the house is enough."

"But when your own house is finished you will have some company," Lawrence pointed out.

"I'm good. I'm not sure I want a pet just yet."

"Fair enough." Cal looked in the box. "Think Clint will want one?"

"Probably. He headed to his place before we did, so he should be there." Lawrence nodded up the road.

"Alright. See you guys at supper." Calvin drove the short distance out to Clint's. He pulled up and honked, a few seconds going by before Clint emerged, pulling his shirt back on.

"I was just about to hop in the shower. What is it?"

"Got you a gift." Calvin reached into the box and held up a puppy. "Want one?"

Clint's face relaxed into a smile as he walked towards the truck. "That sandy colored one is cute. I'll take that one."

"Good man." Cal handed the puppy over.

"Random gift, but thanks."

"Stumbled across them headed into town earlier. Figured we could all use a little company around here."

"You keeping the last two?"

"I'm hoping Annie and Henry will take one off my hands."

"Probably so. Henry was saying he could use some company for when Annie's not home."

"Perfect. I'll be sure to give her one tonight. I'm assuming they're coming to the dinner."

"Just Annie. She said she probably wouldn't stay long but she was too curious about this new vet tech not to come."

"He wasn't so bad," Cal admitted.

"Oh yeah? You met him?"

"Today. Took the pups in for shots. He seems nice enough."

"Good deal. Maybe Al will finally be able to relax a bit."

"Not sure if that's possible."

"You two hashed out your... dilemma yet?" Clint narrowed his gaze at his older brother and Cal nodded.

"Nothing's changed. Just friends."

"I see." Clint, looking a tad disappointed, stepped back from the truck with his new puppy. "Alright, I guess I need to get this little one set up and prepare myself for a decent meal. See you in a bit."

Cal lifted his hand in a small wave as he headed towards his own house. "Not bad." He looked down at the two remaining puppies. "Only two of you left. I thought I'd have a harder time convincing everyone to take a puppy. Guess you guys are just too cute." He stuck his hand in the box and petted soft little heads before reaching for his phone and dialing Annie.

"Hey, sweetheart, give me just a second." Annie's voice turned muffled, her hand over the speaker, "I don't care, Henry, it's what the doctor said to do. Now do it." A rustling sound filtered through the line. "Sorry about that, Calvin. Now what can I do for you, honey?"

"Well, I was hoping you would like to take a puppy off my hands."

"A puppy?" The distaste in her tone had him muffling a laugh.

"Yes."

"What would I do with a puppy?"

"Give it to Henry."

"You mean give it to my husband who just recently had hip surgery. A puppy that will teetee all over my house and new rugs? Calvin, honey—"

"Just think, Annie, it would give Henry some company for when you aren't at the house."

"I'm always at the house."

"Now, we both know that's not true. Weren't you, Alice, and Julia planning a girls' trip to Fort Stockton?"

"Cal, if I bring that puppy home, who is going to let it outside to piddle if I'm not at home? Henry still has another week before he starts physical therapy."

"I'll do it."

"You cannot be dartin' to town every five minutes."

"Alright." He gave up. It wasn't ideal to have two of the dogs, but he'd make it work. He didn't have the heart to take them to the shelter or leave one without a home.

"Thanks for thinkin' of me, sweetie. I'll see you at dinner."

"Yes ma'am." He hung up and glanced at the clock on his dash. He'd take a quick shower and head to Graham's. Perhaps he could convince Alice to take the extra puppy.

H

Chapter Twelve

"No thanks." Alice lightly patted Calvin's cheek. "But I'm glad I was second choice after Annie."

A bit glum, Calvin sighed. "Well then I guess I will have two."

"You're keeping them both?" Julia asked, fluffing a fresh salad. Graham stood next to her slicing cucumbers and tossing them in the bowl as she worked.

"Might as well."

"Leave it to me," Julia told him. "Before the end of the night, Annie will want one of those puppies."

"Oh really?" Alice turned to look at her friend. "You're not going to try and convince me to keep one?"

"No. You're too busy to own a pet."

Alice opened her mouth to respond but realized Julia only spoke the truth. "Maybe Jimmy will want one. He's moving here and all. Might be nice to have some company."

"A worthy alternative," Julia agreed. "But I think Annie and Henry need one more."

"Well, speaking of Annie, she just rolled up." Alice looked up at Calvin. "You better go help her unload."

"What is she bringing?" Julia asked.

"I don't know. It's just Annie. She always brings something."

Everyone peeked out the screen door and sure enough, the petite woman was pulling a laundry basket loaded down with food containers.

Calvin hurried out the door and down the front steps, lifting the basket just as her hold was slipping.

"My hero." Annie beamed proudly as she strutted her way to the main house. "Graham!" she yelled, looking over his porch. "These gardenias are looking pretty sad. When was the last time you fertilized them?"

Graham glanced up from his chopping duties, his face blank.

"I thought so." Annie tsked her tongue. "I'll do that before I leave. Cal, just put the basket there."

"What all did you bring, Annie?" Julia asked.

"Oh, just some snacks for the boys. I told you, I've been on a baking spree. The church kids are having a bake sale this weekend, so whatever extras I had after evenin' out the dozens, the boys are gettin'." She handed a plastic container full of sweets to Cal, his name written in bold sharpie across the lid.

"You spoil us, Annie." He kissed her cheek and she flushed as she walked Graham's container over towards his coffee pot and set it on the counter.

"You know I love you boys. Now, Julia, what can I do?"

"You can sit at the table with a glass of wine and keep us company. Graham and I have the cooking under control."

"That sounds lovely." Annie heaved a tired sigh as she sat next to Alice. "I saw your new young man."

Alice's brow rose. "I'm intrigued. What new man?"

"Your vet tech."

"Oh. Right."

"He was over at the feed store chattin' with Philip. He's a handsome young man." She winked at Alice. "Seems close to your age."

"Not looking for romance at the office, Annie." Alice took a sip of her wine.

"Smart girl. And good. Because I was thinking about introducing him to Ruby." Annie grinned as Lawrence and Hayes walked into the house. "Boys, good to see your handsome faces all cleaned up." She turned her cheek for them to give her a kiss as they removed their hats and hung them by the door.

"There's a red pickup pullin' in. That the new guy?" Hayes asked.

"Yes." Alice stood and walked to the door, waving Jimmy towards the house. "His name is Jimmy. Be nice."

"I'm always nice," Hayes muttered as he sat at the table. Julia walked a beer over to him and he smiled in thanks. Lawrence waved away her offer and opted for a glass of tea instead.

"You have a fever, honey?" Annie asked.

Lawrence chuckled. "No ma'am. Just craving something a bit sweeter."

"That's what a woman is for, Lawrence," Annie stated and had the brother almost spitting out his tea.

Annie chuckled. "Speaking of sweet things." She handed Hayes and Lawrence each a container of sweets. "Now I expect at least a few of you to show up at the church on Saturday and support those kids' fundraiser."

"We will." Graham walked over to his infamous list of things to remember and made a note. "We'll make a donation from the ranch."

"Good man." Annie stood as Alice and Jimmy walked into the house. "Hi there, young man, I'm Annie." She extended her hand and Jimmy politely took it. He smiled in greeting at Julia, his eyes sizing up each of the brothers as they did the same to him.

"Hey, whose pickup is out front?" Seth's voice drifted into the house as he did, and he stopped in his tracks. "Oh, new guy. You're Alice's new punching bag, huh?"

Alice, in response, punched Seth's shoulder and he grimaced. Jimmy laughed. "I sure hope not." He shook Seth's hand and then made his way around the room to meet everyone.

"Sorry I'm late!" Ruby, tucking a stray hair behind her ear, bustled into the house carrying two pies wrapped in cellophane. She accepted Lawrence's help as he retrieved them and set them on the counter. She brushed her hands over the front of her pants. "Phew! What a day."

"Hey, darlin'." Annie gave Ruby a hug and then introduced her to Jimmy. Alice watched to see if there was any instant attraction on either of their parts, but she didn't sense any. She did, however, catch Lawrence's watchful eye on the two of them. *Interesting*, she thought.

She felt a nudge at her elbow. "Don't stare so hard. You'll embarrass him," Calvin whispered.

Alice smirked. "Does Law have a thing for Ruby?"

"I don't know. It's none of my business. He may just be protective. You know how he is."

"Calvin, right?" Jimmy asked.

Cal nodded and shook his hand.

"You get rid of all those puppies?"

"All but one. I plan to keep the last one. Want one?"

Jimmy laughed and then sobered. "You're serious?"

"I am. Annie wouldn't take one, so I have an extra."

"Man, I would, but I don't even know where I will be living yet. A pet might complicate that."

"Speaking of living arrangements...." Alice blinked her lashes at Calvin and feigned feminine adoration.

"What do you want?" he asked.

"I was thinking, if Jimmy is looking for a place and he doesn't want to live in Sheffield, he could rent out my place."

Jimmy's brows rose. "The little house behind Sloppy's?"

"That's the one," Alice smiled proudly. "Cal's been fixing her up for me. If you're interested, I could show you the place," She offered.

"Well, yeah, that'd be great. One less thing to worry about. Is this you offering me the job?"

"Oh, right. First things first." Alice laughed at her own mistake. "The job is yours if you want it."

"Awesome. Definitely."

Annie clapped her hands. "Well, that is worth celebratin' and the perfect reason for a fine meal. Where is Clint and Philip?"

"Clint was going to shower last I spoke to him," Calvin answered. "Not sure about Philip."

"He was wrapping up at the store when I drove through town," Jimmy explained.

"Oh good. Then he'll probably be here any minute. You owe him a big hug, Alice Wilkenson, for recruiting Jimmy for you."

"He posted a flyer, Annie."

"Yes, he did. I don't recall you doing that."

Alice's cheeks turned pink at being scolded. "Fair enough. I'll give him a big hug and my deepest gratitude."

"And another puppy," Cal offered.

"No, Annie's going to take the puppy," Julia stated.

"I'm sorry, I'm what?" Annie looked to Julia in surprise.

Julia pointed to the box where the two remaining puppies slept huddled together. Annie walked over and her demeanor softened. "Well, darn it," she mumbled, reaching into the box and lifting one out. She cuddled it a moment and put it back, then repeating the process with the other one. "Which one is mine?"

Calvin turned astonished eyes on Julia and she winked at him.

"Whichever you like, Annie," he told her.

"I'll take this black one. Henry will enjoy cuddling the little—" She peeked under the tail. "guy."

"Looks like you get the runt of the litter." Seth picked up the last puppy and handed it to Calvin. The spotted puppy nuzzled into the crook of his elbow and continued sleeping.

Alice studied him as he gently brushed his large hand over the small puppy's head and ears. She felt a warmth spread through her chest at his sweet attention to the little orphan.

"Think you could stop gawkin' and help me with the chicken?" Julia whispered in her ear.

Alice jumped to attention and swatted her friend's arm as Julia bit back a laugh. Graham, his eyes amused, didn't say a word, for which Alice was grateful. Alice carried the tray of pan-fried chicken breasts to the table, the men hustling towards their respective seats. Jimmy accepted the seat next to Seth, the youngest brother finding a friend in the newbie. Philip walked into the house.

"Always amazed at your perfect timing, Phil," Hayes teased.

Philip grinned. "It's a gift. Clint's behind me. He was collecting eggs out back."

Surprise had Graham's brows raising. "Since when does he collect eggs?"

Julia and Alice exchanged a look.

"Maybe he's just wanting to help you out since he knows your busy in here," Julia offered with a smile and kiss to his cheek.

They heard Clint walk in the back door and wash his hands in the mudroom. "Hurry up, Clint! I'm starving!" Lawrence yelled from the table. Annie swatted his hand at the outburst.

Clint walked in and sat, his eyes settling upon Jimmy. "New vet tech?"

"Yes sir." Jimmy reached across the table and shook his hand. "Nice to meet you."

"Likewise."

"Alright, let's pray," Lawrence directed and avoided the second swat from Annie.

"Patience is a virtue, Lawrence Dean. You best remember that." Annie's serious face split into a smile as she nodded towards Graham to say the blessing. When the oldest brother had finished, food was passed around the table.

Alice sat in silence as she watched the brothers and her friends embrace Jimmy as a long-lost friend. The Hastings family never ceased to surprise her when it came to welcoming people to Parks. For them to live so far out of town, they always supported the community. The church fundraisers, building projects, other farmers and ranchers, new faces in town, businesses, etc. The brothers kept a hand in everything to make Parks as welcoming as possible. She knew one of them would make an appearance at the church to represent the ranch, more than likely Calvin or Philip, but at least one of them would show their support.

Calvin seemed to pop up in town more often than he used to. Most of that was due to his working on her house, but she noticed his attempts at trying to take a breather from the ranch more often. It was good for them to get off the property every once in a while. Graham seemed to be the only one that could stay on the ranch and never leave and be content with that, though Julia had opened up his world a bit more since her arrival.

"Penny for your thoughts?" Calvin whispered next to her. She hadn't realized she was staring at her friend and Graham as they interacted over their meals.

"Just thinking about you guys."

"What about us?"

"Just that y'all are a pretty wonderful family." Alice turned to face him. "I don't tell you guys that enough… or at all," she chuckled softly. "But y'all really are an amazing family."

Calvin's eyes softened at her compliment. "You're a part of it, you know? You and your dad."

"I know. And I count myself fortunate." Their eyes held a moment, that now familiar buzz starting to surface in the air between them. Alice watched as Cal's gaze darted to her lips and back up again. He offered one of his charming grins before turning back to his meal. She wasn't wrong this time. Calvin was thinking of kissing her. She knew it. And still, after the humiliation of last time and the denial on both their parts, she wanted him to.

∞

It was a nice break from fence work. Rotating cattle from pasture to pasture gave all the brothers a nice, needed time-out from driving posts into the ground and stringing barbed wire. Calvin knew he could speak for the whole lot and say his arms and back needed a rest. However, as he shifted in his saddle, he had to admit he missed a cushioned seat on a piece of equipment versus a horse. Hayes, as conditioned and natural a cowboy as they came, galloped past to cut off three cows attempting to divert from the herd. Cal brought up the rear with Seth. It was the dirtiest position, but Cal didn't mind. Not today. He'd stayed up late with his puppy. He wondered if the other brothers faced the incessant whining that he had and what they did to remedy it. He was exhausted and dragging, not his typical work mode.

Thank goodness for Hayes and Lawrence taking care of the rogue cows. Graham was testing out his new work horse that Hayes had diligently been training for months. The beast was stubborn, and Graham was currently tugging on the reins to pull him in the correct direction, frustration written all over his face. Clint drove the feed truck up ahead. He'd been impressed by Clint's willingness to jump into tasks the last few days. He was more than willing to ride along today, which was not his typical response to cattle work.

"I'm so hungry I could eat one of these cows. Think Graham would notice if I snuck off with one and had a feast fit for a king?" Seth rubbed his rumbling stomach. The man was always hungry.

"You know Graham, he'd notice a cow was missing in the middle of a storm, much less on a pretty day."

"True." Seth adjusted the reins in his hands. "So what is your plan after this?"

"Not sure. Why?"

"Well, it's the weekend," Seth pointed out. "You workin' on Al's house?"

"Probably, especially since she won't be there to interrupt."

"Oh right, the girls' trip to Fort Stockton."

"Yep."

"I'll help you, but it will be after I eat lunch and after I take a nap."

"You sound like a cat."

Seth grinned. "Lawrence's puppy is rubbing off on me."

"How's yours?"

"Whiney."

"His too. They probably miss each other."

"More than likely."

"We should bring them all to Graham's tomorrow and let them play with one another."

"Are we scheduling play dates now?" Calvin laughed.

"Might as well, not like I got anything else going on."

"Speak for yourself."

"Annie would be in a fit if you work on Alice's house tomorrow, it being Sunday and all."

"Well, I plan to. And it will be after church services, so Annie should be appeased."

"I doubt it. At least let her feed you, that might take some of her sting away."

They breached the gate into the new pasture, Calvin hopping off his horse to close the gate behind them. The cattle were all successfully moved into a new grazing pasture, and he saw Graham's shoulders relax as he hopped off of his horse and handed the reins to Hayes. Graham had officially had it with the new work horse. He walked towards the truck and hopped in with Clint, not even wanting to ride the horse back to the stables.

"That ain't good," Seth snickered. "Hayes will be upset with himself, Graham will be annoyed, and that horse better whip into shape or he'll be sold at the first opportunity."

"He didn't do too terrible for his first cattle job. Just needs more practice."

"I reckon it can't be easy having a big man like Graham on your back. I'd be cranky too."

Calvin trotted his horse towards the stables and dismounted in time to hand his reins off to Lawrence. "I've got this," his brother offered.

"Thanks."

"Figured you'd want a head start to head to Al's place."

"Plannin' on being up there the rest of the day. If you get bored, I could use the help."

"Maybe. I might head to Slop's for lunch. I'll check in with you afterwards."

"Sounds good." Calvin slid into his truck and headed towards town. The drive into Parks was always a chance for him to collect his thoughts. When working on the ranch, his mind stayed focused on the work at hand. Most days. But the familiar drive to town allowed him to relax, decompress, and let his thoughts wander where they may. At the moment, he was going over what tasks he wanted to knock out at Alice's house. The AC had been converted to central air and heat. He'd modified the window that once held the window unit, and he'd replaced the back door. The porch needed repainting after it was releveled and set. He might have Lawrence work on that later. His focus would be repairing the kitchen cabinet doors that were struggling to stay on their hinges. Then he'd move onto the next task. "What the—"

He pulled in behind Julia's red car parked out front of Alice's house, surprised to see Annie on the front porch, a floral scarf tied around her head, and planting flowers in pots. Julia, her hair pulled up and away from her face, held a piece of sandpaper in her hand as she worked on smoothing out the new porch railings. The front door was propped open with a paint bucket and music blared inside.

Julia glanced up and smiled. "Hey, Cal."

"Is this the girl's trip?"

"Oh honey." Annie waved him off. "Been to Fort Stockton and back already. Like my new scarf?"

She patted her hair before digging her hands into the potting soil bag by her feet.

"What are you ladies doing here?"

"Same as you, I suspect," Julia grinned. "We are working on Alice's house to prep it for Jimmy. Alice is inside painting."

"Painting?"

"Yep. We picked out colors at that fancy hardware store while we were out and about," Annie told him. "That way Alice was able to pick her own choices instead of you painting everything white."

Cal didn't respond. Instead, he walked into the house carrying his tool bag. Alice stood on a ladder, denim cut-off shorts frayed at the edges mid-thigh and a white tank top already splotched with dots of the blue paint she used on the wall.

"Secret Cove," she called out over the music.

Calvin walked over to the stereo and noticed it was his from his shop. He wasn't sure when she'd swiped it, but it made him smirk. He turned off the booming baseline. "What?" he asked.

"The color. It's called Secret Cove."

"It's nice."

"Lighter than the previous color. I think it opens up the room." She turned then and flashed a smile.

"I was planning on painting this weekend."

"I know. I looked over your list. Finally."

"I see." He shoved his hands in his pockets as he watched her finish the wall and place the roller in the paint tray on the plastic covered floor.

"I also bought new rugs for all the rooms. Talked with Jimmy, and he said he didn't have much in the way of furniture, so I'm going to slipcover the couches and keep most of what's here for him. Speaking of which, that dining chair has a loose leg. I didn't have a screwdriver to fix it, but I added it to the list." She pointed to Calvin's clipboard he'd left on the kitchen counter. "Well, what do you think? You're awfully quiet."

Cal rubbed a hand over his mouth as he surveyed her work. "I'm impressed."

"Didn't think I had it in me, did you?" She grinned as she walked towards the list on the counter. "I want to finish the living room and then I'll start on the bedroom. I have a different color for it." He reached out and rubbed his thumb over her cheek, a streak of blue paint smearing on his finger. He wiped it on a bandana from his back pocket.

"Oh." She placed her hand on her cheek and rubbed the remaining paint away. "Messy work."

"You've recruited good help." He nodded towards the porch.

"Yes, they insisted on helping me today. Annie said the outside looked like death had passed over and that she'd see to it that the flower beds were rejuvenated. Julia just jumped on one of the tasks on the list. Said she'd knock out the porch so when you got here you could stain or paint it."

"Smart choice. Though Lawrence is coming to help me. I thought about sticking him on the porch work."

"Works for me." Alice walked toward the refrigerator and grabbed a bottle of water. "The AC works fantastic. I have it turned off right now because I have the door open for paint fumes, but it felt awesome inside when we arrived. Thanks for that."

"No problem."

"I also saw the new faucets you bought for the kitchen and bathroom. Fancy stuff."

"I thought they were nice."

"Oh, they are." Alice looked around the small home. "I almost want to move back in myself," she grinned.

"You don't hate me for working on your house?"

"No. And I never did hate you, just so you know." She looked at him with kind eyes and he felt himself take a step closer. She didn't back away, but instead, tilted her face to look up at him.

"Good." His voice barely above a whisper, he gently wound his finger around a loose strand of her hair, his knuckles lightly brushing her cheek in the process. "This is a good look on you." He tugged on the strand as he nodded towards the sloppy bun on top of her head.

She flushed, but he felt her fingers close over his hand and lower it to his side. Instead of releasing it, she threaded her fingers with his and squeezed it. "Thanks."

He started to walk away but he felt her hand tighten on his. "You can't tell me you don't feel something different between us. Right?"

"Al—"

"Don't Alice, me." She sought his gaze, forcing him to look at her.

"Okay, yeah, there's something," he admitted. "But I don't know what it is, and I don't want to screw it up. So... just let me process it."

She nibbled her bottom lip to keep her smile at bay.

"I wondered if you were thinking about it." She stepped closer to him and removed his cowboy hat, setting it on the counter.

"What are you doing?" Cal asked, eyeing his hat and trying to remember if he even combed his hair after his shower.

"I'm busting a move on you Calvin Hastings. Again. Now what will you do about it this time?" Alice closed the distance between them, her arms wrapping around his neck as she stood on her tiptoes to lock her lips against his. He stumbled back a step from the sheer enthusiasm behind her seduction. Wrapping his arms around her waist, he leaned into the kiss and felt his heart race beneath his chest. He was in trouble now.

H

Chapter Thirteen

"Lawrence, you take a gander at the paint inside the house," Annie ordered, her gardening gloves and apron stained with soil. "Alice has the porch color all picked out and set aside. Just ask her which one it is, and you can get started."

"Yes ma'am." Lawrence tipped his hat towards Julia as he climbed up the front porch of Alice's house. When he walked through the open door, he paused on the threshold and let out a low whistle.

Alice jumped at the sound, her thoughts completely wrapped up in the moment with Calvin. He'd actually kissed her back this time, and boy, could the man kiss. There was no denying the chemistry between them now. Everything about him felt right. And though Lawrence stood in the doorway, Alice was the one who had to break away. Calvin didn't notice or seem to mind the presence of his brother. He looked stunned a moment before realizing they had an audience.

"I, uh... was just here to get the paint for the porch. Don't mind me." Lawrence grinned as he ducked his head and grabbed the first two gallons of paint he saw and hurried outside.

Calvin rubbed a nervous hand over his face and Alice let out a small giggle that had him flashing her an embarrassed smile. "So?" she asked.

"So..." Calvin replied. "I think we should talk about this."

"But not right now," Alice finished.

"Sooner than later, Al."

"Yes. I totally agree," she grinned. "But we should probably intervene with Lawrence first or he's going to paint my front porch Seafoam Green."

"Shoot." Calvin hurried towards the door shouting for Lawrence, Alice laughing from inside her kitchen.

What had just happened? She rubbed her fingertips over her lips and liked that she still remembered the feel of Calvin's kiss. Her heart still rapidly beat in her chest at the thought of it and the feel of his arms around her. Had Calvin always been so strong? She couldn't quite remember seeing him that way, but she liked the hard press of his chest against her and the strength in his arms as they wrapped around her. Definitely a new sensation, and one she wanted to explore even more.

Lawrence darted back inside and placed the paint buckets back where he'd retrieved them. Alice pointed to the correct ones and he winked at her as he grabbed them and hurried out to his brother.

Julia walked inside and her sly smile had Alice blushing from head to toe. "So... how we doing in here?" Julia asked.

"Good." Alice grinned. "Excellent."

"Oh?"

"Smugness is a good look for you," Alice commented.

"Thanks." Julia fluffed her hair. "I was going to get my nails done, but smugness is easier to maintain."

A guffaw of laughter fluttered in the doorway as Annie heard the last of Julia's comment.

"Where's the guys?"

"Ruby stepped out back of the restaurant with fresh cups of tea. They went to fetch them. I think Calvin needed a good cooling off." Annie wriggled her eyebrows and Julia laughed at Alice's embarrassed pink cheeks.

"Well, he's not the only one."

"So? What now?" Julia said. "Obviously there *is* more than friendship between you guys if you're mugging down here in the kitchen."

"Yeah, I guess you could say that. We're going to talk about it later."

"How do you feel, sweetie?" Annie asked, gently brushing a hand over Alice's hair.

"Good, Annie. Really good."

"I'm glad." Annie pulled her into a tight hug. "Can't say I haven't wanted one of those boys to snatch you up for years. I'm glad it is Cal."

"Slow and steady, Annie. Let's not get ahead of ourselves."

"Oh, honey, you know if Calvin sets his mind on you there is no turnin' back." Annie winked at her. "Whether you like it or not, Alice Wilkenson, you've got yourself a serious man out there."

"Yes, I know." Her eyes drifted out the front door and she watched as Lawrence, no doubt teasing his older brother, cheerfully slapped Calvin on the back as they walked back towards the house. "But let's keep quiet about this until he and I have time to sort it all out."

The men walked in with extra styrofoam cups and handed them to the women. "Thank you, sweetie." Annie took a sip from her straw and sighed. "That is just heavenly. I don't know how Ruby does it, but she makes quite an elixir."

"Slop definitely has the touch," Lawrence agreed.

"*Ruby*, Lawrence. Her name is Ruby. Best start remembering that."

He held up a hand that he understood as he took a sip of his own drink.

It seemed no one wanted to discuss the elephant in the room, and Alice could see the awkwardness in Calvin's movements as he tried to busy himself looking through his toolbox. Before she could stop it, a nervous giggle escaped her lips before she started laughing.

"Uh oh, Al's lost it. Cal, I think you broke her." Lawrence surveyed Alice with uncertainty.

Cal smirked but said nothing.

Alice draped her elbow on his shoulder. "I'm sorry. I just... everyone is so nervous around us right now, and my nerves are shot as well." She shook her hands to relieve the tension.

Cal grabbed one of her hands and brushed his thumb over her knuckles. "Guess you could say Al and I are going to see about testing the waters."

"'Bout time." Lawrence patted his brother on the back. "I say we all eat at Slop— I mean, Ruby's—" he corrected under Annie's watchful eye. "to celebrate. Julia, activate the phone tree."

"Oh goodness." Alice rolled her eyes. "Let's not make a huge deal about this, Law."

"Why not?"

Alice looked up at Calvin to gauge his opinion on the matter and he shrugged. "You know how they are, Alice. There's no talkin' them out of it."

Lawrence cheered as he, Julia, and Annie already started walking towards the restaurant, Julia dialing Graham on her cell.

"You realize everyone in town will know after this, right?" Alice asked.

"I'm counting on it." Calvin kissed her forehead. "I've decided you're my girl, Doc Wilkenson. I sure hope that's alright with you." He slipped his arm around her waist and pulled her close to his side. "Now, let's go make the town gossip.

∞

Three Weeks Later

"If you boys don't stop it, someone's going to break a leg." Annie watched as Clint dove towards Seth and missed the plastic flag attached to his belt loop and the youngest brother ran the football to the goal line set in Graham's yard. When he scored, Seth's victory dance caused everyone to laugh. Cal bent over, hands on his knees to catch his breath. He looked to the porch and Alice shook her head in disappointment. She raised her arms at him, and he bit back a laugh at her competitive spirit. Seth had bested him *and* Clint to score.

"Get it together, Cal!" Alice yelled.

Julia toasted towards him as Graham slapped him on the back. "Don't take it too hard. Al's a beast when it comes to sports. We all know it."

Calvin straightened to his full height. "Well, it's our ball now. We'll see who's left in the dust this time."

The brothers lined up, Cal as quarterback received the snap from Hayes. He diverted his gaze over Seth's shoulder causing his younger brother to dart to the right just enough that he could spiral a pass down the middle towards Philip who jumped in the endzone. Thankfully, the 'football field' was just the length of the yard, so Cal's throw made it home, straight into Philip's awaiting hands. Philip caught it with ease and grinned before flaunting the ball in front of Seth's face.

"They're all really terrible winners, aren't they?" Julia asked as she watched Graham give Philip a shove towards the line and snapped the ball from his brother's hands to try and get his team lined up to score against them again.

"The worst," Alice said.

"Good thing they didn't act that way in high school. Annie would have strung them up and wore them out," Henry chuckled as he shifted into a more comfortable position in the porch chair.

"Need anything, Henry?" Alice asked.

"I'm fine, darlin'. Just fine." He beamed as he nodded towards the men acting like fools before them. Brotherly rivalry on open display.

"You're right. I would have. Now that they're all grown, they think they're immune, but if Lawrence keeps up that taunting mouth of his, he's going to have another thing comin'."

Henry laughed. "Let 'em be, Annie. Let 'em be."

Alice waved as her dad pulled up and parked next to her work truck. Doc Wilkenson hopped out with Jimmy underfoot. The two had been on calls together most of the day. Jimmy watched as Philip tackled Graham to the ground, the oldest brother not even able to toss the ball. Philip stood with a satisfied grin and Graham's flag in his hand. He pointed the ball at Jimmy. "You play?"

"Been awhile."

"Well, any help will benefit them. They need another player on their team." He tossed the ball to Hayes as he walked towards a bucket and pulled out an extra flag belt and handed it to Jimmy. "Graham, Seth, and Lawrence are your teammates. Good luck. You're losing."

"Not for long!" Seth shouted and received a shove from Clint that knocked him off balance.

Jimmy grinned. "Bring it on." His teammates cheered at his enthusiasm as Doc Wilkenson sidestepped the game and claimed a rocking chair next to Henry. The two older men shook hands.

"'Bout time you got here, Dad." Alice sat on the arm rest of his chair and draped her arm over his shoulders. "Calvin is slacking out there."

Cal, standing closest to the porch steps, looked up at her comment. "I'm right here, Al."

Doc and Henry laughed as Cal swiped the sweat from his forehead.

"You could offer the man a drink of water," Doc suggested. "He's sweatin' a river, Alice. Maybe he'd do better if he were hydrated."

"The doctor has spoken." Cal pointed in appreciation at Doc. Alice hopped to her feet and tossed Cal a bottle of water. He took a quick drink before having to jump to attention. He quickly handed her the water, the bottle spilling in her hands as he ran and jumped between the ball and Lawrence. Calvin caught it midair and sprinted towards the endzone, dodging brothers as he went. Jimmy swooped next to him, and Calvin spun to avoid his grab. Henry whistled at the fancy move and Cal jumped over the goal line. He slammed the ball down and pointed at Alice, blowing her a kiss.

Julia laughed. "I'm pretty sure that's a rub in the face."

"Yes, it is." Alice crossed her arms and watched as Cal's face split into a wide smile. "A cute one, though." She clapped her hands and let out a mandatory celebratory cheer.

"In your face, Graham!" she yelled. "Maybe pass it to your own man next time!"

Calvin laughed as he ran up next to Graham.

"I forget how competitive Al is," Graham muttered. "Not sure I like her yellin' at me."

"Yelling is a sign of love," Cal explained.

"Better you than me, then."

"I like it. Most of the time." Calvin grinned. "She's a fiery one, my Alice."

"Just don't let her coach little league one day."

"She does seem to have her coach hat on." Calvin winked over at Alice as she continued yelling at his teammates.

"Water break. Water break," Annie yelled. "You boys are about to melt." She walked out to the field with waters and handed them out. "And this is your Annie reminder that you boys are supposed to be playing flag football, not tackling. One of you is going to get hurt."

"We'll be alright, Annie, don't you worry." Hayes gave her a squeeze in thanks.

"Alright team! Huddle up!" Alice clapped her hands and hurried down the porch steps. She waved Calvin and his brothers towards her.

"What is it, Al?" Clint asked, chugging his drink.

"Nothing. Just wanted to say to keep up the good work. Y'all are stompin' them." She smiled proudly as she patted Calvin and Philip on their backs. "Now get out there and don't disappoint me. Victory drinks at Ruby's if we win." She put her hand in the middle, and though the brothers groaned at the childish act, they placed their hands on top of hers and yelled, "Team!"

And a team they were, he and Alice, Calvin thought. They'd always been good friends. They had each other's backs. Calvin tipped his head towards her and planted a kiss on her cheek. "You know, I kind of like having you boss me around, Coach."

"Good. Because it's in my nature to boss people around. Now get out there and win, Calvin Hastings." She gave him a quick peck on the cheek before starting towards the porch.

Calvin grabbed her arm and tugged her back, the momentum slamming her into his chest. He kissed her solidly on the lips and lingered a moment. "You're my girl, Alice Wilkenson." Briefly pressing his forehead to hers, he breathed her in a moment. "Alright, now get. I've got a game to win." Spinning her towards the porch, he accepted the slap on the back from Annie as he ran past her towards the other brothers. Alice *was* his girl, and when he glanced at the porch, her smile was tender and her eyes sparkling as she watched him. Though he questioned why he never saw her this way before, he was grateful he did now. And now that he had discovered Alice was his match, he planned to never let her go.

Continue the story with

Order Here:
https://www.amazon.com/dp/B08B2QZZSB

INTRODUCING THE FAMILY

THE SIBLINGS O'RIFCAN SERIES

KATHARINE E. HAMILTON

The Complete Siblings O'Rifcan Series Available in Paperback, Ebook, and Audiobook

Claron

https://www.amazon.com/dp/B07FYR44KX

Riley

https://www.amazon.com/dp/B07G2RBD8D

Layla

https://www.amazon.com/dp/B07HJRL67M

Chloe

https://www.amazon.com/dp/B07KB3HG6B

Murphy

https://www.amazon.com/dp/B07N4FCY8V

All titles in The Lighthearted Collection Available in Paperback, Ebook, and Audiobook

Chicago's Best
https://www.amazon.com/dp/B06XH7Y3MF

Montgomery House
https://www.amazon.com/dp/B073T1SVCN

Beautiful Fury
https://www.amazon.com/dp/B07B527N57

Check out the Epic Fantasy Adventure Available in Paperback, Ebook, and Audiobook

The Unfading Lands

The Unfading Lands

https://www.amazon.com/dp/B00VKWKPES

Darkness Divided, Part Two in The Unfading Lands Series

https://www.amazon.com/dp/B015QFTAXG

Redemption Rising, Part Three in The Unfading Lands Series

https://www.amazon.com/dp/B01G5NYSEO

Subscribe to Katharine's Newsletter for news on upcoming releases and events!
https://www.katharinehamilton.com/subscribe.html

Find out more about Katharine and her works at:
www.katharinehamilton.com

Social Media is a great way to connect with Katharine. Check her out on the following:

Facebook: Katharine E. Hamilton
https://www.facebook.com/Katharine-E-Hamilton-282475125097433/

Twitter: @AuthorKatharine
Instagram: @AuthorKatharine

Contact Katharine:
khamiltonauthor@gmail.com

ABOUT THE AUTHOR

Katharine E. Hamilton began writing in 2008 and published her first children's book, The Adventurous Life of Laura Bell in 2009. She would go on to write and illustrate two more children's books, Susie At Your Service and Sissy and Kat between 2010-2013.

Though writing for children was fun, Katharine moved into Adult Fiction in 2015 with her release of The Unfading Lands, a clean, epic fantasy that landed in Amazon's Hot 100 New Releases on its fourth day of publication, reached #72 in the Top 100 in Epic Fantasy, and hit the Top 10,000 Best Sellers on all of Amazon in its first week. It has been listed as a Top 100 Indie Read for 2015 and a nominee for a Best Indie Book Award for 2016. The series did not stop there. Darkness Divided: Part Two of The Unfading Land Series, released in October of 2015 and claimed a spot in the Top 100 of its genre. Redemption Rising: Part Three of The Unfading Lands Series released in April 2016 and claimed a nomination for the Summer Indie Book Awards.

Though comfortable in the fantasy genre, Katharine decided to venture towards romance in 2017 and released the first novel in a collection of sweet, clean and wholesome romances: The Lighthearted Collection. Chicago's Best reached best seller status in its first week of publication and rested comfortably in the Top 100 for Amazon for three steady weeks, claimed a Reader's Choice Award, a TopShelf Indie Book Award, and ended up a finalist in the American Book Festival's

Best Book Awards for 2017. <u>Montgomery House</u>, the second in the collection, released in August of 2017 and rested comfortably alongside its predecessor, claiming a Reader's Choice Award, and becoming Katharine's best-selling novel up to that point. Both were released in audiobook format in late 2017 and early 2018. <u>Beautiful Fury</u> is the third novel released in the collection and has claimed a Reader's Choice Award and a gold medal in the Authorsdb Best Cover competition. It has also been released in audiobook format with narrator Chelsea Carpenter lending her talents to bring it to life. Katharine and Chelsea have partnered on an ongoing project for creating audiobook marketing methods for fellow authors and narrators, all of which will eventually be published as a resource tool for others.

In August of 2018, Katharine brought to life a new clean contemporary romance series of a loving family based in Ireland. The Siblings O'Rifcan Series kicked off in August with <u>Claron</u>. <u>Claron</u> climbed to the Top 1000 of the entire Amazon store and has reached the Top 100 of the Clean and Wholesome genre a total of 11 times. He is Katharine's bestselling book thus far and lends to the success of the following books in the series: <u>Riley</u>, <u>Layla</u>, <u>Chloe</u>, and <u>Murphy,</u> each book earning their place in the Top 100 of their genre and Hot 100 New Releases. <u>Claron</u> was featured in Amazon's Prime Reading program March – June 2019. The series is also available in audiobook format with the voice talents of Alex Black.

A Love For All Seasons, a Sweet Contemporary Romance Series launched in July of 2019 with

<u>Summer's Catch</u>, followed by <u>Autumn's Fall</u> in October. <u>Winter's Call</u> and <u>Spring's Hope</u> scheduled for 2021 release dates. The series follows a wonderful group of friends from Friday Harbor, Washington, and has been Katharine's newest and latest project.

Katharine has contributed to charitable Indie Anthologies as well as helped other aspiring writers journey their way through the publication process. She manages an online training course that walks fellow self-publishing and independently publishing writers through the publishing process as well as how to market their books.

She is a member of Women Fiction Writers of America, Texas Authors, IASD, and the American Christian Fiction Writers. She loves everything to do with writing and loves that she is able to continue sharing heartwarming stories to a wide array of readers.

Katharine graduated from Texas A&M University with a bachelor's degree in History. She lives on a ranch in south Texas with her husband Brad, sons Everett, and West, and their two dogs, Tulip and Paws.

Made in United States
North Haven, CT
24 August 2024

56490101R00129